Consider an Island
An t-Eilean Sgitheanach

D1346866

Consider an Island
An t-Eilean Sgitheanach

RHONA RAUSZER

edited by Linda Williamson

Polygon

This edition first published in 2004 by
Polygon an imprint of Birlinn Ltd
West Newington House
10 Newington Road
Edinburgh EH9 1QS

www.birlinn.co.uk

ISBN 1 904598 12 9

British Library Cataloguing-in-Publication Data
A catalogue record for this book is
available from the British Library.

Typeset by Hewer Text Ltd, Edinburgh
Printed and bound by CPD, (Wales), Ebbw Vale

To my sisters
Morag and Cairistiona

Contents

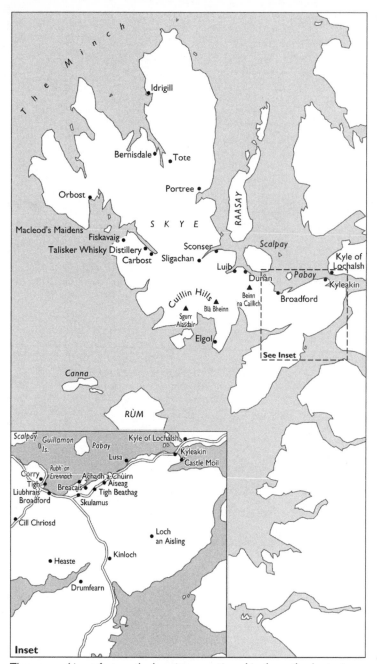

The map and inset feature the locations mentioned in the author's stories

List of Illustrations

1. Voluntary Aid Detachment nurse, 1939.
2. Rhona in the doorway of her great-grandmother's cottage, Breacais, Skye.
3. Rhona, husband Kazik (foreground) and friends sailing, 1964.
4. Lusa cottage, where Rhona lived from 1971–86.
5. Rhona modelling her new gillie shoes.
6. Rhona, BBC Radio dramatist and storyteller.
7. 'Teach Me To Waltz', an original painting by the author.
8. 'Mallaig Fishermen', an original painting by the author.
9. Grandmother Rebekah Mackinnon's original spinning wheel.

Introduction

Consider an Island, An t-Eilean Sgitheanach is a celebration of storytelling, the author's tribute to her ancestral homeland, the Isle of Skye. This selection of thirty-two stories, historical narratives and imaginary tales, represents a third of Rhona Rauszer's extant writings. Christened Beathag Màiri (Rebecca Mary) and born in 1911, the eldest daughter of Marianna Macleod and Christopher Sykes, Rhona inherited not only her Skye grandmother's name and spinning wheel (see 'Skye's the Limit') but also the clan Mackinnon propensity for art. She was creating stories at the age of three, entertaining her mother and the other children of the household: 'I would "Listen to this, Mother!" and wag my finger right up to her face and make her show attention.' Because Father worked with the railways, the family would regularly spend half the year in Skye and half the year in their home in Hoylake by Liverpool. The beauties of the island summer after a winter in the industrial South would surely captivate the imagination of a young child: 'In Kinloch I would cross the river and go up the hill and lie in the heather and lie on my back and tell myself stories, and this is how it all began,' explains Rhona.

The happiest memories of those years growing up on Skye (1914–1930) come from Tigh Liubhrais in Broadford, her Grandmother Rebecca's house, where stories of the forefathers were often told. Rhona's great-great-grandfather was known locally as Duncan Bàn, a descendant of the Macleods of Raasay and highly respected for his ability to read, write letters and help people with their problems (see 'Consider an Island'). When Rhona tells stories today she ascribes her understanding of human nature, honesty and style to him:

> Anything I write comes out of my mind and not out of my brain, and what comes into my head is very little to do with myself and is attributed to my ancestors, to Duncan Bàn in particular, yes, because he's the one I know about that was able to write fluently and talk, a great talker. He was yes, he definitely was, a literate man.

With no formal education, due to the effects of whooping cough at the age of five and a weakened heart, it is remarkable how Rhona's dream to become a professional actress was realised. The film parts assigned to her were admittedly small and rather insignificant (for Denham Studios' *Hungry Hill* and *Odd Man Out* in 1946); but the dramatic work she accomplished for BBC Scottish Home Service was laudable. Contributions to Scottish radio plays began in 1938 (BBC Glasgow's 'Sauchiehall Surround'); and parts in programmes on heritage, Scottish history and Highland Gaelic culture, and in mystery and adventure stories, *Woman's Hour*, and children's and school dramas for radio ran continuously, with contracts for more than eighty different titles, until 1968. After her husband died that year Rhona's broadcasting career shifted from drama work to writing, and she withdrew from the world of theatre and public life to a croft in Idrigill, North Skye.

World War II had been central to Rhona's life: she served first in the Voluntary Aid Detachment in Lennox Castle emergency hospital during the 1939 Clydebank Blitz, and then for five years in the Women's Royal Naval Service. Training on the famous boat the *Water Gypsy* with A.P. Herbert, she was commended for 'amazing endurance' and earned placements on FS *Paris*, HMS *Albatross*, and HMS *Pembroke*, stationed in Plymouth. Throughout the War BBC commissions were honoured, rehearsals attended, and broadcasts made from the Overseas Division (1944). At the tail-end of the War Rhona joined the Citizens' Theatre and performed under ENSA in France and Germany, then in Sadler's Wells. But with the War truly over, she longed for the Highlands and moved north to Scotland, living near her younger sister and mother in Dunblane. There she set up in business with a small antique shop, and in 1947 met her husband Kazimir Stanislaus Rauszer . . . one day a great lorryful of Poles stationed in Dunblane bashed into the French awning of her shop in the cathedral quarter of the city, and the only man who could speak English was Kazimir. He apologised profusely . . . eventually the couple fell in love and married, each with a deep and abiding respect for the other's creativity:

> I got some kind of refinement of speech from Kazik because he was Polish and very eloquent, he was descended on both sides of his family from literate Austrians and Poles (back to 1411) who were well educated; he himself in Grenoble. He had an explanation for absolutely everything. Kazik could spell in English where I couldn't.

It is clear that he had a profound influence on her development as a writer, 'Kazik taught me to see beyond looking,' and his listening ear was critical as Rhona unfolded her stories, gaining the confidence to persevere when first attempts at story writing were refused by BBC Glasgow in 1946. In 1951 'Over the Sea to Skye' was accepted for broadcast for a fee of £6.6s, but Rhona was in demand for drama parts (slightly more lucrative) and she did not take up the pen seriously again until the early 1960s when Kazik took her on a cruise to Orkney and Shetland. Rhona kept a diary:

On the boat it was so wonderful, who wouldn't write at sea, the motion of the boat, the beauty of the scenery and the sound of the waves, and the motion – it asks you to write. The seagulls ask you to write as well, they're fascinating the way they swoop down on the boat. And you're free and relaxed, so wonderfully relaxed.

Her producer AP Lee in Glasgow was impressed with the travel stories; he asked for more and this gave Rhona the encouragement she needed. Of course, along with the opening for work writing and recording stories for BBC Scotland came the reality, the confinement of length and restriction of time. But in true discipline is true artistry.

In 1968 when Rhona moved to Idrigill as a widow, writing stories became a mainstay. BBC Aberdeen were very interested in her work and producer Allan Rogers came often for material to prime his *Town and Country Magazine*:

He would let me know, phone or write a letter and say, 'I'm coming to Skye, can you have anything ready for me?' And I'd say, 'Yes!' And it wasn't a chore, I enjoyed doing it. So I was knocking them back daily really. Some he rejected but not many; he took a good many of them, thirty-eight I think. And then unfortunately the way it stopped – and I stopped because he stopped – he changed his job, he was put onto going abroad and doing articles on tourism. So that was the end of it. I lost my listener. I wasn't going to do it anymore.

In 1971 Rhona decided to leave the croft in Idrigill and move to a seaside cottage in Lusa, a few miles from Breacais in South Skye where her mother's ancestors had first settled in the eighteenth century. The magic of Lusa held the reclusive Rhona for fifteen years and she was happy developing her talent for painting. She sold her lovely, wistful landscapes of Skye and the Macleod Maidens (see story below), evoking the shore at Lusa and Beinn na Caillich for tourists and art lovers. But the wee cottage required upgrading and financial problems grew. To maintain herself Rhona resorted to collecting whelks, and on this activity, an intensive, prolonged searching for shellfish, she blames her loss of sight. In 1986, registered blind, Rhona left Lusa and came to live in Broadford at An Acarsaid with her four-legged companion (see 'Gaynor my Guide Dog').

Blindness has not stopped Rhona's storytelling, however, quite the contrary. There was a gap of about ten years when writing took second place to painting, but the stories were never stopped. In 1981 BBC Glasgow sponsored a competition for story writing, with very strict rules of twelve hundred words 'and no more'. Rhona submitted 'Silver Strands' (see below) and won! And several more stories from her fireside at Liveras Park, Broadford, have been recorded onto cassette tapes and transcribed by friends, during these past seventeen years of darkness. But imagination comes from the heart and so her stories of the Islands cannot stop, as long as Rhona knows we are interested. And this, I have assured my favourite storyteller, is what we mainland, city dwellers of the twenty-first century need most in our lives to hear.

Three of the stories, about magical trees, are set in the Highlands of Scotland; all others belong to Skye, the Western and Northern Isles. The stories have been ordered for reading, beginning with childhood narratives and the 'Ever-Young'; progressing to stories about men and their boats, pipers and gamekeepers; then including a group of women's stories and homely domestic tales; and culminating with the spiritual world of the cailleach and the sacred seer. It is important to remember when reading these stories that they are works of fiction, from oral tradition. The author has maintained her writing is 'common knowledge, based on fact, according to my grandmother and my mother'. The title for the book is derived from the Biblical passage in *Matthew*, 'Consider the lilies of the field . . . they toil not neither do they spin.'

We acknowledge the friendship and help of Angus Macphee (Skye), the invaluable aid of Mrs Christine Martin, the Breacais) for guidance in every aspect of this work; Mr Neil

MacGregor (Edinburgh) a member of the Gaelic Society of
Inverness, for transcripts of the spoken Gaelic; and the
Scottish Arts Council for a grant to develop bilingual story-
telling in writing.

Linda Williamson
Edinburgh, 2004

To School in Skye

Lying on the flat of my back I reached for the bung-hole on the old wooden barrel. Out of it slithered slowly a black sticky liquid which I caught and welcomed with my tongue. 'It was meant for sick cows,' Calum Mór said, and was called molasses treacle. Calum Mór was my aunt's shepherd and could play 'Fly away Peter come back Paul' better than anyone I know, and when you are a puny girl of seven you appreciate things like that.

I loved my treacle but hated my breakfast. Porridge, ugh! And I suppose I was a creature of habit. First, my skinny arms would heave my schoolbag into place, then my sou'wester, and lastly my wellington boots. They were very good for kicking the large dry circles (like treacle bannocks) of cow manure under which the mushrooms grew.

On reaching the gate up on the main road to Ardvasar I always looked inside the large long-legged, wooden mail-box standing drunkenly, half in the road and half in the ditch, like Calum Mór after the cattle sale. Yes, the jar of tadpoles I had put in the night before was still there. And the handles of the newly filled milk cans rattled in the wind, their lids half off, like new calves foaming at the mouth. Three miles still to go, seven peat-bogs still to jump . . . two more gates on the hill road still to climb. 'Awful i-so-lated,' Aunt Curstag used to say, 'and only six pupils' – three cousins, myself and the game-keeper's two brats, Donald and Isa Kelly. I started to sing, 'Donald Kelly burst his belly o'er the heid of jam and jelly . . .' It was all right, they didn't understand English. Lots of the kids in the south end of Skye didn't.

I reached the first gate. There were three long brown snakeskins hanging on it. 'It was an experiment, you see,' my cousin Hamish said, 'if you cut a snake in half and hung the top half in a high place, the tail end would wriggle up and rejoin it in a few days' time.' We were still waiting.

At the second gate there was a tinker's tent. They worked hard for their living. Red Stewart chased us with whatever job was in hand – a frying pan or enamel chamber pot with a hole in it.

I was always first at school because I was teacher's pet. In fact, she wasn't up most days when I got there. So I climbed through the window as usual and put the kettle on for her; then I went and rang the school bell with all my guts. 'Not so loud,' she moaned and got up, scratching herself. I laid out cups and she gave me biscuits with animals on them. Then I watched for the others running up the hill and I formed the head of the line.

One day the youngest, Angus Beag, disappeared before my very eyes like a fairy. I ran down the bealach and stared into the black waters of the peat-bog. Slowly three little white things poked up – they were his fingers. I grabbed at them lying on my belly and heaved with all my might! He went and broke my meccano set lying in bed, all those weeks afterwards.

We carried one peat each to build the school fire and sugar in a tiny mustard tin. At the break I collected sheep's droppings, because the weather was warm, and sold them in little white paper bags to Donald and Isa as cinnamon balls. They didn't know the difference . . . and if they did? Well, a bargain's a bargain, and, I had polished them.

My cousin mended the teacher's bike and at the end of the term we all knew 'Man's Chief End' and 'Doh-re-mi-fa-sol'. And one of us could nearly write. But when the Inspector of Schools arrived one day in a morning-coat and top hat, the teacher was looking very worried and scratching her bushy red hair with a knitting needle. She made us line up in front of the blackboard for questioning. Angus Beag shot his hand up to be excused.

On the way back he'd taken a look at the Inspector's horse and gig, and somehow or other the reins had got loose from the fence. The next thing we knew we were careering down the hill and along the road, tinkers and all after the horse and gig! The Inspector was too flabbergasted to ask us any questions that day, which was just as well; as we couldn't have answered them anyway, what with me having thrown my new schoolbag (books and all) over the bridge and into the river. Well, the river was in spate and they might have fallen in, mightn't they?

Soon after that (there was no time to go to school, anyway) everything was flippity flap. A new baby was born to Auntie Curstag. The gig came crunching down the half-river half-road to the porch of the little farm (nothing growing round it save a little bit of wild honeysuckle). The doctor sometimes came on horseback. He was a very absentminded sort of man. Once he shoved his pipe in his pocket when it was still lit. He tore along in the wind, his jacket and saddle ablaze like one of the Four Riders of the Apocalypse. When he realised what had happened he had an awful job trying to douse himself in the ditch. He needed a wee snifter after that to steady his nerves.

Aunt Curstag and the new baby were in the big room over the barn with the sloping ceilings and the American clock (bought off a travelling Pole who thought he was the wandering Jew). We got Aunt Curstag to put him up for the night to find out if it was true. His face was like a piece of tripe with wrinkles and he seemed ageless, right enough.

Often shepherds spent the night there when they came to help out with the dipping. There was a little middle room for them with a skylight in it. One old boy had need to get up in the night and being shy, rather than ask, had relieved himself through the skylight. The biggest of my cousins didn't believe him and tried for himself; and since he couldn't succeed, he maintained old Fleppen was a liar till this very day.

We played hide-and-seek up the old wooden stairs on rainy days in these old rooms, among some of the nicest furniture I have ever seen. There was a chair made out of an old wooden barrel, and the little cradle had a roof on it, like a chapel. There was a barrel of oatmeal stored on the landing. Angus Beag had hidden there one time and fallen asleep amongst the meal, like a little white lamb with his curly hair all matted. No one could find him for a day and a night.

Another girl cousin came to stay with us once. She was frightened of the shadows from the candles and oil lamps at night, and she got worse when we took her to the window to show her the rats – rats marching up from the river and climbing up on the barrels set ready for them. They contained water and poison, and were covered with fine paper strewn with cheese and titbits. When a large number of rats accumulated on top the paper would burst open, and they'd all fall in, with an unholy screeching and splashing that made the girl cousin cry to go home. She said she was frightened of Germans too. 'What's a German?' I asked her, but she didn't seem to know.

I couldn't help thinking the baby smelled of carbolic soap and reminded me of wash-days, when all the clothes would be taken down to the river. A big fire would be lit, and the clothes would be boiled in an iron cauldron set on stones. The women would ease off their black stockings, and wriggle their toes and enumerate their complaints before tramping the clothes again in big tin baths, and beating the bad ones on flat stepping stones in the river – the water parting on either side of their ashen but ample calves. They would frequently sing and joke at their work, and many a one waved her bloomers to a man as he passed on his way to the peats or the sheep fank.

The day of the christening was the most exciting. The baby got lots and lots of money in its hand, and my aunt pinched it all. Angus Beag wondered how it came to have so many fingers already. He thought they should grow on afterwards, one by one.

Bella the maid got drunk from the dregs left in the wine-glasses and let Iain Mór squeeze her in the scullery. (Disgusting!) There was a huge mountain of a dumpling with sixpences in it. The minister ate so much of it he had to open up his waistcoat to let his belly out. I didn't think he had a hope in hell of ever getting it shut again.

Sometimes I would climb the hill and breathless reaching the top, lie in the heather and try to die. I'd often done this (I still do) especially when they'd been bad to me. Once they'd tried to blame me for burning holes in the mantelpiece in the sitting-room with a red-hot poker. It was my cousin that did it! I was always being blamed for things I didn't do. Why, there were those cups that Bella the maid had brought all the way from Glasgow. They said that I had broken some of them. Well, I hadn't! It must have been the boys. It certainly wasn't Bella either. She had brought them with her as a present, so she just took all the remainder of the cups and saucers, stood on a flat stone in the middle of the river and smashed them, one by one against the rocks. Crash! Bang! It was wonderful. My aunt was furious. She had brought Bella from an orphanage in Glasgow. The girl was still touchy about it and didn't like to be blamed for anything at all.

I'd been for a ride on a pig that day. It's a very difficult thing to do, they're so very wiggly-woggly and you've got nothing whatever to hold on to. Sometimes I walked back along the river with my other big fat aunt. They said she wasn't very well. But I think she was just plain rude. She kept on belching at every second step. She never said, 'I beg your pardon.' I sometimes stayed with her. She lived in the big house.

It was different to my Aunt Curstag's farm, a sort of estate. There were lots of pansies round the lawn and a marvellous avenue of rhododendrons all the way down to the sea. The twin cousins lived here. The girl one had golden hair in plaits that nearly reached the bottom of her kilt. We all ran about in bare feet most days, some for health reasons and some for obvious reasons – the shoes I had were laughing at the toes. The soap they used was a change from carbolic. It was a stuff, some very expensive French soap with a name like 'sheep', but didn't smell of dip. I used to lie on top of a boat that had a canvas cover on it – it made a kind of bed – and dream and dream . . . I was very fond of lying. I sometimes lay on my stomach at the side of the sea and my nose would bleed. I watched it flowing out ruddy and glowing on the out-going tide, making me shudder; reminding me of the time we went with Neilag, the keeper's oldest son, in a small boat to the Island of Seals, and how he'd clubbed one on the head and it had cried out, its whiskers and flippers stiffening. It was a 'grown-up' wickedness, the worst kind of all; I told the minister so and he buttoned up his waistcoat with sheer embarrassment and told me never to cross my bridges till I came to them – as if I could, before!

Once there was a wreck. We had all gone to bed in the nursery, my cousins and myself. It was a terrible storm. Our new governess came in and got us all up to go and look out the window, in case it was the last sight we ever saw of our uncles and my father getting into small boats, and trying to row out to the enormous yacht that was halfway up on the rocks and halfway in the sea, and there were lots of people swimming about. But we weren't allowed to go out of course, and see it all. Next morning we ran hell-for-leather down to the shore. There were mattresses floating on the surface of the water and boxes of eggs and clothing. The tins of condensed milk and jellies were still edible, and we found a box of cigars intact. We lit a fire, and dried these off on hot stones and smoked one or two till we got dizzy. Then we gave the rest to Red Stewart the tinker, who had moved his camp nearer the big house now that the stags could be seen on the top of the mountains and the festive season was approaching. My uncle passing by the camp saw him smoking one of these.

'I see you've taken to smoking cigars,' he said. 'The best, too! Corona-Corona, be damned. Quite a connoisseur. May I offer you one of mine sometime?'

My uncle called us into the gun-room to be introduced to the owner, skipper and crew of the wrecked yacht. They'd all been rescued by my father and uncles. The owner was completely deaf and dumb. It was most intriguing to find out how you could talk to him. Somebody said he could lip-read, so I twisted my mouth into all sorts of directions, but he didn't seem to know what I was saying.

One day when lessons were over in the schoolroom, still stimulated by the excitement of the wreck, my twin cousins and I decided we would risk going aboard my uncle's yacht *Trident*, which was swinging at anchor in the bay. We decided to board her like pirates unseen by any of the crew. The crew were men from the Island of Harris in the Outer Hebrides, four of them. And the trip this day was to the Isle of Tiree. But try as we might we had been unable to find out why it was all so secret, and why we had not been given permission to go.

The idea to stow away came to us when we realised that there would be no lunch at home that day. Iain (the boy twin) said that the cook was having an epileptic fit in the kitchen, and all the grown-ups were milling around her. We were not allowed in the kitchen anyway, so I couldn't exactly say what was going on. But for us everything went as planned. We bribed Neilag to row us out to the boat in the dinghy, and we slithered aboard silently. No one saw us. We hid in an unused sail locker and waited, taking a swig from time to time from a tin of condensed milk punctured with a marline-spike. After some time we heard the skipper taking his place

15

at the wheel. The deck-hands Neilie Beag and Archie brought up the anchor. We were under way. It was pretty choppy when we got out a bit, and we were very cramped indeed, huddled together in so small a space. What's more we would have to wait till after dark, to crawl unseen along the deck on our bellies and drop down into the cockpit, then into the aft cabin, which was never used except when my uncle and aunt were aboard. It contained four comfortable bunks leading off a saloon.

The night was stormy. There was a big swell on and the seas were riding high. We began to feel lonely and frightened and guilty, to say nothing of seasick. We had started to undress and snuggle down in the bunks, having shared out the last of the food we had brought with us, when we noticed a large box-thing standing in the middle of the saloon. We dared not have a light on so it was not easy to make out exactly what it was. We decided to creep up and have a closer look. One of the twins raised the lid a bit, and the moon shone through the porthole on the marble features of a handsome bearded man. He was quite dead. It was a coffin with a corpse in it!

There we were then, alone in the middle of the night with the wild water of the Minch tossing and tearing at the boat. We threw ourselves at each other like in a rugby scrum and tried to blunder towards the cabin door but it had jammed, or probably we had jammed it in our striving to get out. We began to panic and started an almighty screaming and yelling, but no one came. Surely they could hear us. We continued to scream, screech and holler till we did get the door free, then tumbled up on deck to find the skipper and crew down on their knees, having armed themselves with

Bibles and shotguns and the like, and calling upon the Almighty to protect them from the small pigmy figures emerging from the cabin below. 'O, a Thighearna 's an Dhia,' (God protect us!) they shouted in the Gaelic, taking us for banshees or evil spirits of some sort, leaving the corpse and making towards themselves. Imagine their astonishment when they came to sufficiently, to realise it was only us! Their relief was so great that they allowed us to spend the rest of the night with cups of cocoa and chocolate biscuits in the warm forecastle, on the knees of Neilie Beag and Archie.

Next day the corpse was respectfully placed on its native soil in Tiree, and we were thrashed with enthusiastic vigour by my father on our return. My uncle never thrashed anyone. He was a sort of God, to be loved and at the same time feared. The tinkers all loved him, and round about the New Year he used to drive round in an open Mercedes and hand out hot turkeys swathed in straw and packed in hat boxes, and deliver them himself to their tents.

My aunt had a different approach. She had been known to line all the tinker children up in a row and delouse them with what was known as a 'dust-comb'. They sold them at the little shop at Isle Oronsay together with some paraffin and cotton wool she needed to collect the livestock with.

There was one old girl who bought one of these combs and the next day brought it back to the shop. 'It's no good,' she said. 'Why can't you give me one like I got the last time?' And in the Gaelic, 'Bheireadh e mil' air a h-uile sgriob,' which means 'it would take a million in the one swipe'.

Once the winter was over we would think about getting back to the farm in time for An Earreigh (the Spring), and the lambing, the time when motherless lambs were brought in to suck from the bottle held in the strong fingers of Calum Mór, the fingers that were sometimes called Òrdag and Lùdag,* and sometimes Peter and Paul. And the whole world would begin again, round and round like the cramachan churning the butter when we would earn (for the loan of a good forearm) a bowl of stapag (meal with sugar and cream) and I could lie once more under the old wooden barrel and catch the treacle with my tongue.

* Òrdag and Lùdag – names of the thumb and first finger; the others are named Fionnlagh Fada (chief long stretch), Mac an Aba (abbot's son) and Déideag (little fair one).

Three Fat Fishes

My mother was never one for going for walks (as such). If she had energy to spare (and she had plenty) she would use it in the garden, which she loved, or have some definite purpose, perhaps someone sick to visit or to see a house for sale. She didn't believe in just stravaiging about aimlessly.

So it came as a bit of a surprise when she said one day, 'Come on, put your coat on and we'll go for a walk!' She took me to a place four miles or so away, taking a rough hill track past stacks and black sinister bogs no longer worked, half hidden by mosses stained crimson and pink and intoxicating-smelling heather and myrtle whose roots seemed to strangle each other . . . 'It's a shame,' she said, 'when you think of the price of coal these days, but then there's no one left to work the peat any more.'

'Who do they belong to?' I said.

'They used to belong to three old ladies who lived in a cottage down here.' And we continued down the rocky path till we came to the sea again.

I knew this place quite well for it was one of the prettiest in all the Outer Hebrides, a dream place with its ancient crofts and the sound of the looms in the distance like an army of soldiers advancing in tackety boots. The fishing nets were draped over thatched roofs like hairnets, and the seagulls squawking over-all. There were real hens that nested in trees, their wings unclipped, and cattle that munched their way right up to the doors of these primitive fishermen's cottages.

'There it is then, that's the one they lived in,' said my mother, 'but it wasn't like that in their day though; much of it is tumbled down, but Cairistiona, Catriona and Ealasaid were well off. You see they had been left quite a large legacy. Their brother had gone off to Australia, sheep farming . . . "Alec's gone out with the merinos" they would say, and sure enough he had made a packet out there with this new strain of sheep . . . and he was generosity itself to those three girls.'

'Weren't they old women?' I said. 'I think I met one of them when I was small. She made me open my mouth . . . "Show me your teeth," she said. "Uh-huh, not bad! Are they your own?" "Yes," said I. "Well, see that you keep them then!"'

'Oh, that's very typical of Cairistiona,' said mother, 'she lived quite a long time after her two sisters and got very cranky towards the end. You see, they had been extremely beautiful in their young days, and their brother kept sending them lots of jewelry, silver teapots and silk dresses, and satins and shawls galore; there was hardly room in the cottage for all the fine things they had accumulated, and when he died they were worth quite a fortune, and every lad from far and wide would come courting them. But the trouble was they were terribly vain! (And you take a lesson from this, my lass.) They turned their noses up at every eligible suitor who called on them. But there were three young men who were pretty persistent.

Finlay was Catriona's boy and he loved her to distraction,

but she would have none of him, him being only a crofter. Seoras was only after Ealasaid's money, but he kept trying and would have made her a very good husband. And Duncan, Cairistiona's boy, that was sad . . . they eventually did become engaged, but she kept him dangling so long that he went off to sea. For as he said, "Distance makes the heart grow fonder. Maybe you'll have me when I get back." But he never did get back. He was drowned you see in a storm off Newfoundland.'

'Poor Cairistiona,' I murmured.

'Well, there they were then, the three of them dressed to kill and fast growing older, relying now on rubbing beet-root to their cheeks to bring the colour back and all sorts of other tricks. (It was even said that they collected urine to wash and bleach their hair; it was used in these parts for softening the tweed too, if you can believe all you hear.) Indeed, they were becoming the laughing stock of the place as spinsters often are. "It's no use," the fishermen would say to each other, "it's no use your trying your luck with them, or throwing your hook in their directions. It's three fat fishes those ones are after, and, believe you me, they'll get no more than the wind of a fresh herring if I'm not very much mistaken, for if they don't make up their minds soon they will be lucky if they get any catch at all." But they couldn't make up their minds, and as time went on their behaviour was just pathetic. No one ever called to see them now – no men that is. But they were far too vain and silly to let their few remaining women friends know this. So what do you think they did?'

'What?'

'They would send away for tobacco and cigars and the like,

even black twist, and burn it in the room before letting anyone in to see them. Then, in a great pandemonium and flutter they would rush round emptying glasses, and opening windows pretending to let out the smoke, then sit demurely, hands crossed on their laps and greying heads of ringlets discreetly hanging to hide their modest blushes. They would start confidentially apologising, whispering through heavily bejewelled fingers that it was "John" you see, or "a Sheòrais" or "a Sheumais" that had paid them a visit and had just left. "So sorry," they would say, "I hope you don't mind . . . Now would you be taking a cup of tea? Or maybe a wee drop of something to keep the cold out – port wine, it's awful good for the stomach." '

'Oh, Mother, stop it! I don't know whether to laugh or cry.'

'No, my dear, and neither do I.'

Tha Mairi anns an leabaidh
Tha Mairi cho tinn
Cha tig i as an leabaidh
Gus am faigh i gu tea
Mar a chan mise facal
Bithidh bat' air mo dhruim
Tha Mairi anns an leabaidh . . .
Tha ise cho tinn.*

Mary's so ill that she can't get up
And she won't get up, until she gets her tea,
And if she doesn't get her tea
I'll get the stick on my back!

* An old Gaelic song that Mother used to sing. My mother wanted
me to know about these three because we were related, they were
cousins on her side. And because I was vain, I used to act in front of
the mirror (I finally did become a small-part actress), it was always
in my blood to act and dress up. And my mother used to take the
mickey out of me and tell me, you know I must be sensible, 'or
you'll wind up like the *three fat fishes!*'

Dougie and the Ducks

They called him a snotty-nosed little brat and nobody had any time for him. So he had been tossed from pillar to post, from home to home. He was a foundling, you see. His father was a drunk and his mother had died when he was still a very small child. So into foster homes he went, from one foster home to another and there was nothing really attractive about him – perhaps his hair – he had rather beautiful hair, but apart from that he was an ugly little twit and so badly behaved.

It was a nightmare trying to bring him up. He was tossed into one foster home after another and the reports sent to the headquarters were always the same, that this boy was very difficult. He had an insatiable desire to play practical jokes on everyone; some of them were extremely disagreeable, like putting clingfilm over the lavatory seat in some of the houses where he stayed. One dear old girl, a foster mother who was very kind and very sweet to him, had the habit of putting paper curlers in her hair at night. One night Dougie had crept up behind her with a box of matches and set alight all the papers. You could hear her screams for miles.

So that's the sort of lad he was; but they bore with him and the Church was good, and the Boys' Brigade were kind, and when he grew older he joined a group of hikers, and they used to go to Loch Lomond which was not all that far from where he had been born, in Dumbarton near Glasgow. And so he would go off on these wonderful hikes round Loch Lomond, and even over to Arran climbing, and this did him a lot of good and through time he had made enquiries about his parents. He found out that there was only one living relation that anybody knew about and he was in the Isle of Skye. He was a brother of Dougie's mother, so he would be an uncle, and Dougie always had the secret ambition that he was going to hike as far as the Isle of Skye and look for his long lost uncle, and see if he could live with him. 'It would be a darn sight better than living with all the foster parents,' he thought.

So through time he equipped himself with all the sorts of tin pans, hiking boots, haversacks and tourie bonnets and everything that was required on such a trip. He had been left a little money in fact and so off he went starting on his own, through Dumbarton and along Loch Lomond. On and on he went getting further and further north and staying at youth hostels, and staying anywhere he could find: in barns and under haystacks and hedges, and being an absolute menace on almost every step of the road. When he was going through Dumbarton, for instance, he stopped at the bridge – and you could always see there lovely swans, ducks and wild geese. Of course Dougie had to pester them and would throw stones at them and things like that. He was really a pest! Eventually, however, after many many days of walking and many nights of sleeping rough, he got as far as Kyle of Lochalsh and then over to Skye. There he was told that he did indeed have an uncle who had recently died, but *he* had one son called Angus who had retained the croft. He was living alone in an enchanted place miles from anywhere, down by the sea, not very far from Kyleakin itself. So Dougie made for this house. He was never reluctant about going to anybody's house whether he knew them or not. He was rather like a little stray dog who would lift his leg at any gate-post or threshold where he thought he could make a stance and claim some kind of help or could seek some kindness. So, eventually he got to Angus's croft.

Young Angus was a charming lad and everybody adored him. He was quiet and never bothered anybody. He was very much a recluse living there with his music and his animals all round him, his dogs and his sheep, a few cattle and a boat; but his most prized possession was his fiddle, which his father had handed down to him from his grandfather and his great-grandfather. So it's not surprising that Dougie got a great fàilte, or welcome, from his cousin Angus. He was taken in and given a good meal and a very warm welcome, and Angus told him he was very happy to put him up as he had no help on the croft. The lambing was about to begin and an extra pair of hands would be more than useful. So Dougie felt very confident and settled in immediately, being a very arrogant sort of fellow.

(You see, this, in my opinion, is often the way when no one loves you and nobody cares for you: you seem to make an extra effort to make yourself felt.) In fact, Dougie had barely finished his meal when he started nosing around, poking into everything, opening drawers and turning over papers. Then his eyes fell upon the fiddle which was hanging on the wall. He grabbed hold of it and took it down off the wall.

Now this did irritate Angus who stopped him and said, 'No, no, no, give me that because that is my most precious possession. My father gave it to me and it has been handed down for generations and indeed, it is supposed to be a Stradivarius would you believe it!'

'Huh!' said Dougie, 'that's nothing – I've got a cousin who's a chemist in Glasgow – so I have.'

Well, Angus just laughed that off and very carefully put the fiddle into its proper case which he had underneath the trust, a wooden sort of couch which was always to be found in these sort of crofts. He tucked it away reverently and said to Dougie as a sort of compensation, 'Well, I've got a bicycle, would you like to have a spin around on that? I could take you up to the lochs tomorrow. There is one loch that I am particularly fond of and I go there a lot. I take my fiddle and play to the ducks and the geese there, and on a sunny day it is very soothing just to sit and watch the movement on the water as the ducks make those enchanting circles, getting wider and wider until they reach the reeds, and at this time of the year it is quite possible that there will be some young. They are so pretty. I am sure you would like to see that.'

'Huh!' said Dougie, 'I don't know about that. How far away is this loch?'

Angus said, 'Well, Loch an Aisling, that means "my dream loch", is only about a quarter of a mile away up the hill there.'

'Can I take the bike up there?' said Dougie.

'Well, no,' said Angus, 'you would have to walk part of the way but you could take the bike for a mile or two, then leave it and we would walk the rest of the way.'

'Oh, all right then,' said Dougie, 'we'll go tomorrow morning.'

And so they did with a packet of sandwiches tucked in beside Angus' fiddle in the case. Angus carried his case and Dougie took the bike and rode ahead, and slowly they went up towards Loch an Aisling. Dougie was only a few yards ahead of Angus when they got there. He had dumped the bike in a ditch and started scrambling up to the loch. It was not long before Angus caught up with him and found him standing with his mouth hanging open staring at a bundle of female clothes: 'There must be someone here, there must be someone, there be some female swimming in the loch!'

Angus peered around but could see no one at all at first. Then he thought he saw something swimming under the water making its way towards the reeds. It was the form of a lovely creature, a beautiful woman's form. He was very embarrassed of course and turned round towards Dougie to say, 'Come on, let's get out of here, come on, run down the hill, we'll get away from here, we don't want to embarrass anyone!'

But, meanwhile the miserable Dougie had whipped the fiddle out of its case and stuffed all the lady's clothes into it, and was halfway down the hill before Angus could stop him. He ran and ran with Angus running after him holding his fiddle under his arm. There was no way he could catch up with him because he had mounted the bicycle and was away down and round back to the cottage. Angus was miserable and followed feeling guilty, dejected and wretched, and because of this mood he walked slowly along the road trailing his feet.

At last he got home and opened the door and went in to see Dougie standing in front of the mirror over the mantel doing the most extraordinary thing. He seemed to be pulling out his hair; and then Angus realised his hair was actually coming out, and in handfuls and falling to the ground. 'Good gracious me!' said Angus, 'what on earth is happening to you? Was your hair real?'

'Of course it was real!' said Dougie, 'what kind of a man do you think I am that I would have artificial hair at my age?' Dougie walked over to the fiddle case and opened it. 'It must have been the clothes I touched. There must have been some sort of poison in the clothes I touched.' So he opened up the fiddle case to find that the clothes were no longer there, and in their place was a huge bundle of beautiful soft, downy feathers in all shapes and sizes. The case was absolutely full of feathers! Would you believe it?

They were both so terrified they didn't know what to do, and Dougie being the coward that he was immediately started to grab all his clothes and pulled a woollen bonnet over his now completely bald head and collected his haversack and all his possessions. He ran out of the house to make his way to Kyleakin and get the ferry across to Kyle of Lochalsh and make his way back to Glasgow, leaving poor Angus dumbfounded and completely shocked and at a loss to know what on earth to do next. So, after a wee dram, as he had a little drop in the kitchen cupboard left over from his father's funeral, he got all his courage together, got ahold of the fiddle case and made his way bravely up the road again very, very slowly. In fact, before he reached the base of the hill it was already darkening and beginning to cloud over and hide the sun.

The golden sun was putting magical streaks around the edge of the black clouds which seemed to form themselves into human shapes – or perhaps they weren't human. Perhaps they were angels with great long wings coming out at either side of the black clouds, wings of gold and halos of gold. He thought, 'Oh Lord, I am seeing things, it's all mad, this never happened, this can't be true.' So he sat in the ditch and opened up the fiddle case to make quite sure that he wasn't dreaming the whole thing, but sure enough there were feathers galore.

So he took them up reverently and laid them at the side of the loch where the clothes had been found. He said a little prayer and turned on his heel and saw nothing more of the shadows under the water. There was nothing there but a beautiful, big gander swimming about as usual, one or two geese and some other birds that he couldn't distinguish in the half-light. At the edge of the reeds there seemed to be a very large bird, perhaps a swan – a lovely looking creature – it could have been a Canadian goose but he wasn't very sure and he didn't hang around to find out. He got home as soon as he could and put his fiddle back in the empty case, said his prayers and went to bed.

Now he didn't hear from Dougie for a very long time, but eventually he heard about him. He heard that he had become a reformed character. Evidently, the fright he had got up in Skye at Loch an Aisling had just done the trick, and had converted him into being a very reasonable character, quite a decent sort in fact. He had made a bee-line of course for his cousin in Glasgow who was a chemist, and between them they tried out every potion and every medicine and every hair-growing stuff the chemist could lay his hands on. Through time Dougie's hair did begin to grow again slowly. It seemed to be keeping pace with the improvement in Dougie's character. When he behaved better so his hair grew thicker until eventually it was curly again, a big mass of curly hair.

He got a job with his cousin who was a chemist in Glasgow and sometimes he would still go hiking. He would hike up to Loch Lomond and he would linger over the bridge at Dumbarton and quite often he would see a large, beautiful bird, but it wasn't alone. There was another bird with it and they were strange birds. They were different to any he had ever seen, but in some strange way it would come to his mind that he had seen one like it up in Loch an Aisling in the Isle of Skye.* He could not help wondering if the other one could by any chance be his cousin Angus, and indeed, 'What on earth happened to the fiddle?'

* Loch an Aisling – the dream loch is found by Ben Aslak near Kylerhea Glen.

Island of the Ever-Young

She stretched out her long skinny legs, and her ice-cold feet felt for the warmth that came from the small bundle huddled up on the end of the bed – it was her youngest brother, Neil. There were three of them altogether, two boys and herself, and they were all sleeping in the one bed. The other bed was end to end with this one. Their mother lay in it, and she was crying and sometimes moaning out loud. The midwife tried to stop her, and got quite cross with her at times. "N ainm na naoimh, bi sàmhach!' (In the name of the saints, be quiet!) she would scold.

Giorsal would quickly close her eyes and brush away her own tears. How could anyone sleep when there was a new baby just about to be born? Her mother had told her long ago, as far back as the day before yesterday, that she could expect a new baby brother or sister, she was carrying it around inside herself for a bit, just like Bellag the cow before she had the calf; but Bellag the cow didn't have all that pain . . . Giorsal began to think her mother might die, so, rising to her knees on the straw mattress she clasped her hands and prayed to the Almighty. Just then there was the sudden sound of a baby crying out from nowhere. It was a miracle. Her prayers had been answered. It was true, then, this almightiness of prayer. She had proved it for herself.

Turning on to her back again she stared up at the yellow

stains of damp that made patterns on the ceiling. Sometimes she could see a goat's face with a long beard like old Fergus Ruadh. No wonder they called him The Goat. Sometimes dozens of eyes seemed to wink and drop tears on her . . . but perhaps there was a leak in the roof. She fell asleep towards morning and dreamt she was on a swing tied to the old apple tree that had been struck by lightning, and a great gust of wind came and swung her up and up till she landed in heaven, and God was there, sitting, on a golden throne, and He had two white doves, one on each knee, and He gave her one and said, 'Take that to the baby, and come back for the other one for yourself;' and she swung back through the clouds and put the dove on her mother's knee beside the new baby, and her mother smiled the lovely smile, and pushed her long black hair aside from her breast to feed the new baby. And Giorsal knew she must go away, but she didn't know where; and then she woke up and left her bed with her brothers still sleeping in spite of the noise of the slop pails being carried up and down the wooden stair and the poit mhùin being emptied. She crept silently over the floor and down the wooden stair, and ran outside in her bare feet and semmit to look for the cat.

'Pushag, pushag,' she called softly . . . She must be hiding somewhere. She looked in the barn, and there – hidden in the hay was the yellow cat with a litter of new kittens – imagine, on the selfsame day her mother had the baby!

She ran to the corrugated iron scullery where the previous night's milking had been put in setting bowls and stole a couple of ladlefuls and took it back to the kittens, then slunk back to the house for her own porridge. She had nearly finished when Eoghan Fergus the shepherd came in.

'That damn cat's been at the cream again! Passed her licking her lips outside the barn just now.' He barged towards the pantry and came out in a towering rage, 'Stad thusa, just you wait you filthy vermin! I'll wring your neck,' and he marched off towards the barn lifting a nearby hay-fork.

Giorsal slid quickly down from the high wooden trust and beat him to the barn door. She just had time to throw a handful of hay over the nest of new kittens, and hide herself, when in came Eoghan kicking over buckets and throwing the hay about; then he saw the cat, and raising the hay-fork in the air slew the writhing animal to death. Giorsal's screams could not be stopped till she choked and vomited. Meanwhile, Eoghan found the kittens and thrust them into a sack; and slinging it over his shoulder he marched down towards the river, Giorsal flinging her slight body in front of him every step of the way and tearing the skin off his knees* in an effort to stop him. When it was done and a heavy stone submerged the sack, Giorsal put her hands to her ears to dim the sound of his cruel laughter – a sound she knew she would never forget – and she felt a strange feeling of 'almightiness' inside of herself, and she used it against Eoghan and all his family.

Two years passed before she realised her power had worked again, during which time Eoghan had gone to America, emigrated and got a job on a building site working on top of one of those skyscrapers. The scaffolding had given way, and he fell to his death at the early age of twenty-two.

* tearing the skin off his knees – attacking him vigorously with words (Sl)

When they brought his remains home they could hardly believe their eyes. He was all dressed up in evening clothes and patent leather shoes, stuff he had never had on in all his mortal days. Giorsal could feel no sorrow at his parting, but vaguely she hoped that was the end of her 'almightiness'. But no, two weeks later when coming home from school, she met Eoghan's father down on the shore tarring his boat. She decided to be kindly and friendly, chat him up a bit. She was secretly afraid of anything bad happening to him too.

'Latha briagha,'* she said.

' 'Se gu dearbh,† a bit warm for working, though,' said Fergus Ruadh. 'And I've still to go up the hill. There's a fox been working at the lambs. I'll need to set a trap for it.'

'I've never seen a fox. Are they really such dirty, wicked animals?'

'Destructive buggers, all of them,' said Fergus, reaching for a jagged-looking iron ring.

'Ach, I don't believe you, and you're surely never going to use that iron snare on it?'

'I will that, I'm telling you; you can come and see for yourself if you like!'

'Very well then,' and she followed him with a vague hope of doing something to prevent him snaring the fox. They walked for miles up the shoulder of the mountain. It was all Giorsal could do to keep up with him. He was a short man, who made up for his small size in sheer brute strength. (The men said that he could lift up to two hundred pounds in the one hand.)

* latha briagha – fine day
† 'se gu dearbh – surely

For part of the way there was a rough path, more like a burn, with miniature boulders in it, and it was hard going for the fragile girl. She tried to walk on the soft white clay between the rocks, till, after a mile or two they left the sore track behind, and all the scratchy dead bracken and scorched heather, and were climbing from rock to rock with harder ground beneath them. Occasionally they would come on patches of loose gravel and Giorsal would lose her footing and slide or fall her own length down again. Always Fergus Ruadh kept a pace or two ahead of her, except when he would find a fox's lair. They were unmistakable, usually under a sheltering slab of rock and lined with flattened out grass and fern and littered with the naked white bones of lambs, rabbits and birds, all strewn about, and here and there a tuft of matted wool or a lonely feather.

It sickened her to look, and she said she wanted to go home. She began to feel the time must be passing seven as the sun had already reached the peak of Beinn na Caillich, staining the sky blood-red as it hid down behind the mountain. What would she tell her mother? 'I'm going back home, Fergus,' she said.

'Don't be daft, girl, keep on a little yet! The fox gets suspicious if you lay the trap too near its den; take him unawares, play him up at his own game. There's a ridge here that he'll be coming over and we'll get him on the hop.'

'Don't do it, Fergus, please don't do it!'

But he continued eagerly. As Giorsal trudged behind him she became more and more exhausted. Pressure came into her ears. 'It must be the height,' she thought. She felt her eyes blurring, and she hated Fergus Ruadh. Following in his every foothold made her dizzy. Did she see his feet slowly changing shape, or was she imagining things? She thought his tackety boots* looked more like hoofs and his legs had gone bent and thinner. His coarse crotal, brown tweed jacket seemed hairy, yet smooth like fur. Sometimes she would see him sideways on, and a glinting green eye would cast a glance at her. She began to freeze and pinched herself and put spittles on her eyelids to bring herself awake again, like she did in church, when suddenly he turned full on her; his face and the backs of his hands were covered with red hair, his eyes green and shiny, like wet herrings at night. The fear of death came into her.

'Am béist ruadh, the werewolf!' she yelled as he ground his teeth and stretched his long claws out towards her, and she stumbled backwards against a jagged rock that pierced into her back; and just as she thought she was done for she got the 'almightiness' again, that feeling of strength and challenge, and she spat in his hairy face and ducked her body low to the ground, then rolled out of his reach, then somersaulted down the mountain-side swinging from boulder to boulder like a roebuck on the run. She dare not look to see if he came after her. Down . . . down . . . down she tumbled, till she reached the lower ground. She tore her clothes and flesh as she barged her way blindly through the silver birches, rivers and dykes, finally collapsing in a wet, cold faint on the kitchen floor.

Her mother lifted her up and tried to make her stand. Slowly coming to she recognised her father. She hadn't seen him for two years or more. He'd been away at sea. She heard him arguing with her mother.

* tackety boots – hobnailed boots

'Now wait till she's better,' he said, 'don't bully the girl till you find out what for!'

'I'll thrash her anyway, for the time of night and the state of her clothes,' said her mother reaching for the long, five-fingered tawse that hung on the nail on the wall. (She'd never used it on Giorsal before, only the boys, but this was too much: she'd need to have a pretty good explanation before she'd let the girl off with this.)

But then Giorsal didn't really mind if her mother wanted to thrash her. Many a time in the past she would rather it had been her that got thrashed than the boys. She stood ready for it. Then her father put his big seaman's hand on the top of her head, and in a commanding voice said to his wife, 'Leave her alone, woman!' And just then there was a shuffling at the door. The latch was lifted slowly, and in walked Fergus Ruadh. Giorsal let out a strangled scream as she clung to her father, burying her face in his double-breasted jacket.

'Och, och, so that's it. Gu dé as ciall, a tha thusa ag iarraidh?' (What the hell do you want?)

'That's a fine way to greet your friends. I heard you were back, but it's not that I'm about. It's your lassie there. Didn't she follow me up the Bealach Mór.* I let her come, mind you. I could see no harm in it. She was that determined to stop me trapping the fox. But then when I thought she had climbed far enough and the sun was down, I got worried for her, and turned in my track to tell her she had better be running off home on her own. Well, she took one look at me – I never saw anything like it – you'd think I was Mic an Sad†

* Bealach Mór – big hill pass
† Mic an Sad – Son of the Devil

38

himself, hoofs an' all,' and he began to laugh harshly (as his son had done when he drowned all the kittens).

Giorsal ventured a keek at him from under her father's arm. It was Fergus Ruadh all right, as he was before, just a stupid old bumailear of a man, completely harmless.

He leaned towards Giorsal and said, 'Did you think I was going to take a poke at you, a skinny wee thing like you, without so much as a curve or a cioch showing yet? Me that never got the chance to lay a woman since the Boer War?' And the two men laughed heartily, and sent Giorsal up the wooden stair to her bed.

'Did my mother thrash you?' whispered Seoras her brother.

'No.'

'You fly bitch, you always wangle out of it.'

'Keep quiet, there,' yelled her father, 'or I'll come up with the stick to you all!'

'You and who else?' squeaked little Neil, rolling himself up in the blankets at the foot of the bed.

In the morning there was a terrible racket going on. Fhearchar, Fergus Ruadh's only remaining son, was hammering on the door like a lion. Giorsal dragged herself from the bed, stiff and sore from the previous day's exertions, and went to open it, but her father had got there first. He was standing in his long johns* and shirt, and giving Fhearchar a hell of a ticking off for wakening him.

'Wait a minute,' said Fhearchar, 'you've got to hear what I have to say. I'm worried and I need your help. It's my father, you see, he's beside himself, mach as a rian, stark raving mad.'

* long johns – men's long-legged underwear

39

'Speak with more respect for your parent, lad, he's all you have!'

'Dhia beannaich mi,* do you think I don't know that?'

'What's wrong then?'

'Well, he was over here last night, wasn't he?'

'Yes.'

'Was he all right – not drinking – or anything?'

'Not a drop, more's the pity. I drank it all myself, the minute I left the ship (the cailleach doesn't like it in the house, you see). Come inside! You'll give me my death of cold standing there.'

'No thank you, man, I can't. I'm wanting you to come over with me as quick as you can. My father's pouring good whisky down a rat hole by the side of the fireplace. He says there's an awful stink coming from it.'

'Dia, he must be mad!'

'And last night he didn't go to his bed at all. He carried the three sacks of potatoes, all we had to put us through the winter . . .'

'Eh!'

'Yes, he carried them, one at a time, up to the river, opened them and chucked every single potato into the river, one by one. He said they were stinking, and had been poisoned.'

'Bi falbh, get away with you, man! It's not Hogmanay: you wouldn't be trying to fool me?'

'No, as sure as I'm standing here, as sure as death!'

'Well then, it must be rabies. Did he get bitten by a mad dog, do you think, or did he get a bang on the head?'

* Dhia beannaich mi – God bless me

'No, no, neither. Come on, man, hurry! I'm wondering
. . . would you stay with him while I get the doctor? . . . Ah,
maybe I could get a loan of your horse?'

'On you go, boy, leave it to me . . .' and he was already half
into his trousers.

'I'll take a – well – it might be wise to take a rope. Is he bad
enough for that, do you think? I know he's devilish strong,
obh obh, gu dé a nis (what next)?'

Giorsal watched them as they walked to the barn for the
rope. And she watched them as they caught and bridled the
long-tailed tan-and-white horse that she had named Pease
Brose, because that was the colour of it, and big tears ran
down her face; because in her heart she knew it was all her
fault. She knew, too, that she would never see Fergus Ruadh
again, and she was right, for they took him away to Inverness
and he never came back.

Some months later, she was watching her mother dressing
the baby in front of the kitchen fire. She was holding it out to
warm its bottom, and had spread *J G MacKay's Catalogue* on
the floor to catch the droppings. Giorsal turned away towards the window in disgust. Her mother noticed that she
was staring stiffly as though at something in the far distance.

'What is it?' she said, 'what do you see that's gripping you
so?'

'They're carrying a coffin down Fhearchar's croft,' she
said, 'and there's another one waiting at the foot of ours.'

'Don't be daft, girl! There's no one dead. Fhearchar's in
good health, and carrying on fine since his poor father was
taken away. He's a good lad, and you'd do well to favour
him.'

'It's funny he's not taking a cord, then. He must be the

41

dead one himself . . .' (Giorsal continued as though she hadn't heard her mother speak.) 'It's my father in front, and old Domhnull Uilleam has the next cord. It's our own Seòras that's leading the other coffin – that's funny! There's sixty or seventy people in all . . .'

'Giorsal, Giorsal, 'an ainm a Dhia* . . . stop that!'

'. . . It's starting to rain. Wee Neil's hiding in the ditch . . . I think he's crying . . .'

'Come away from that window, you frighten me!'

'Come and see it, Mother . . . they are moving off, now.'

Her mother pushed the baby into the wooden cradle and moved towards the window angry, yet afraid . . . afraid of what she might see, but when she looked out there was nothing – only the withered apple tree – its branches stark and naked in the sun. And that night when she'd got them all to bed, she sat with her husband alone and told him the way of it with Giorsal. But he showed no surprise. It was as if he knew about it already.

'The sins of the Fathers,' he said, 'unto the third and fourth generation.'

'What do you mean?'

'It's been handed down . . . the second sight . . . Nighean Mairi an Seer.† Mairi an Seer was my Si'-Si'-Seanmhathair.'

'Your Great-great-grandmother?'

'That's it. She was burned as a witch in Urray near Beauly.'

'Why did you never tell me?'

'I was afraid it would come between us . . . that you wouldn't want me . . .'

'Foolish man.'

* 'an ainm a Dhia – in the name of God
† Nighean Mairi an Seer – the daughter of Mairi the Seer

'And I didn't really believe in what she said.'

'What did she say?'

'Well, they have it that she put a curse on a man called Fergus. He was her lover, and had grown tired of her, so he had her burned for a witch. There's many said she never was a witch, but that he just wanted rid of her. However, it's said that so great was her love for him that even as she cursed him with her last breath, she took part of the curse on her own line:

"Fergus, son of Eoghan, son of Fergus," she said,
"When all my charred bones lie deep in nettles,
"And ninety-nine years are done,
"Then will I take three of yours for one of mine,
"Then, and only then, will my spirit rest in peace!" '

'Dia beannaich sinn.* It's terrible . . . terrible.'

'O, mo ghaoil,† dry your eyes.'

'It's happening now – Eoghan in America, then Fergus, and then . . . and then . . . what Giorsal saw . . .'

'Uist! Be quiet now, fan sàmhach.‡

As time went on Giorsal grew into a pretty fine specimen (if a little delicate), good colouring, black hair and blue eyes, and the kind of figure even old Fergus would have admired, had he been alive. Mind you, there's no doubt about it she was strange, especially with animals. They would all come to her, eat out of her hand, instead of her going after them. Even the weasels down on the cladach would jump at her and

* Dia beannaich sinn – God bless us
† mo ghaoil – my dear
‡ fan sàmhach – stay silent

43

she'd come to no harm. She'd play games with them as she gathered the sea pinks* that grew on those queer shaped patches of short, green grass that the sea had separated from the land. 'Dangerous,' her father said it was down there, 'especially on a high tide,' but she took no heed. The cailleachs seemed to think it was high time she had a click.

'What about you and young Fhearchar?' they'd say, jabbing her in the ribs and winking. It's true, it wasn't easy to avoid meeting him at the peats, or when she took the meal and water gruel or buttermilk to the men shearing the sheep at the fank, and lately he'd taken to waiting for her down at the well, when she came to draw the water. Fhearchar was easy to look at and easy to love, but she knew he must never be for her. She could never undo what she had already done. She knew that to love him would be to destroy him, and she kept her distance. She wasn't aware that her seeming indifference only enticed him the more.

'Can I carry the buckets for you, Giorsal?' he said one day when he felt he must speak his mind (he'd had about enough of waiting).

'No, you can't!' And don't come near me if you value your life,' she replied (pretending it was a joke). She splashed water at him for the hell of it, then knelt down to fill the buckets. He slid his arm round her waist and lifted her hair from the back of her neck to kiss her bare shoulders. 'No, Fhearchar, no, please no,' she pleaded.

* sea pinks – very purply-pink little flowers; they grow on little islands of short grass, because the sea sometimes goes over it right down on the shore, and they're absolutely beautiful. They don't last long if you start picking them or trying to take them home, but they're so delightful to look at! They're just like clover really only vivid pink.

'Why not? I'm sick of just looking at you.'

'To tell you the truth, I'm afraid for you. Bi falbh. Off with you!'

'It's afraid for yourself you should be!' he said, and kissed her again taking her strongly in his arms this time. And she knew there was nothing more she could do about it. She was far too much in love altogether. 'Say that you love me, Giorsal!'

'I do, just now, but I'm afraid for what I might do to you, if you should come to hurt me.'

'Dia, you sound like a witch.'

She sank to the ground and spoke to him as though to herself . . . 'That's the trouble. I think I am one. I'm afraid, afraid of the feeling, the sensation of that almightiness that freezes me, destroying anything I should look at in anger. Don't let me think about it now . . . now that I love you, and you *know* . . .' and he held her tightly while her small body shook with sobbing, and a great love grew between them, and he knew that he was now sharing her terrible almightiness.

That night there was a full moon, bright as day, and Fhearchar had made her promise to meet him down at the end of the croft by the Craobh Gealaich – the Moon Tree – so called on account of the number of couples who had trysted there, carving their initials and little hearts on its crumbling bark. Giorsal traced them with her finger and wished she had a knife to cut her own and Fhearchar's names. She was fidgety, she had got here too soon . . . far too soon. Fhearchar would hardly be through milking the cow yet, and she had forgotten he had to make his own food (she'd soon put that right). She had better run down to the cladach for a bit, to while away the time. She could think of nothing but Fhearchar, and hoped that by the time the stags had cast their horns this year she might be his bride. She would make good food for him, and care for him well, after all she owed it to him . . . Wasn't it her fault that Eoghan and his father . . . there she went again, oh God! When would she be free from this thing . . . this feeling . . . this terrible guilt?

Crossing through the long, sharp grass of the machair she dropped down on to the sand, and made footsteps across the damp, massive furrows the ripple of the tide had made. It was like walking on a giant's forehead. As she walked she came to softer sand that didn't hurt the bottom of her bare feet so much. It was sinky, though, and made her feel a bit scared. She had meant to go and have a chat with the weasels on the Green Island when she noticed that there were other footsteps ahead of hers. They were the same size, and she found that if she pressed one foot firmly down – or sideways – the foot in front would do the same. She tried to catch up with them to see if hers fitted into them, but she couldn't reach. Then she tried her other foot, and the matching foot in front did likewise. It was terribly exciting, and she found she couldn't stop. Splosh . . . splosh . . . splosh splosh . . . splosh . . . splosh. She took bigger strides; so did her other feet. She now knew that they must be hers, and gradually she began to see her other self walking in front of her, and she kept on following herself, and there was a great noise of the sea moaning around her, and she thought she heard voices, then one voice . . . someone was calling her name . . . It sounded like Fhearchar.

'I'm coming!' she shouted, 'coming . . . com . . . i . . . n-g,' but she found she couldn't turn round, and the wind and salt

46

sea spray was choking her, and dragging at her clothes, dragging her on and on and on till she felt like a feather soaring through an airy space. Sometimes she would be dragged back according to the way of the wind, and a hand – was it the hand of her other self – would reach out to her again. Now she could feel its grip, solid and real. Was she perhaps in two worlds at the same time? She was well beyond the reach of the pounding waves now, and there was a long slit in the sky that seemed to widen. A dove flew out of it. It was the dove, the one God said she must come back for and it led her towards the light, through millions of twining, swirling rainbows full of light and colour, dazzling her so that she couldn't see properly any more, and she began to freeze with the awful 'Almightiness', till suddenly the bird settled on the back of her hand, and her whole being filled with a new, warm glow.

Fhearchar waited by the tree, and his blood was boiling. If he didn't love her to distraction he would call her a bitch. Hadn't he nearly dragged the tits off the cow's udder at the milking in order to be here on time. He'd hardly eaten a bite either. He was still licking the bits of aran coirc (oat-cake) from between his teeth. She must have gone down to the cladach; she was always going there. Or had her father put a stop to them straightaway? It would be just like him. Well, he would try the cladach first.

He ran down through the machair calling her name. It would be all over the village now that he was courting her – Ach, who cares – 'Giorsal! Giorsal? . . .' he shouted, and his voice echoed deep down in the huge sea-worn cavities of black rock frightening the white doves that nested there, and making them take to the wing. 'Giorsal! Giorsal! Where are you?' He thought he heard a reply, or was it just the whistling of the wind amongst the machair reeds? He could see for miles across the sea – right to the edge of nowhere – or was it America? (Giorsal's father said it was.) 'Giorsal! Giorsal! . . .'

Wait. What was that floating on the water? Something white and pink . . . God Almighty! Is that not what she was wearing? . . .

He threw himself into the water not caring a hoot that he couldn't swim; then tried to reach her. He was in to his neck, and his wellington boots had filled and were heavy. He was near, though, and it was her all right. He gave a leap out of his depth to reach her hand, and as he caught it and tried to regain his footing, an immense tidal wave took them both, and a dark cloud covered the moon leaving the whole place in the blackness of the night – or so they said, those that found them next morning – when the tide went out. They were lying on a little green island amongst the wild sea pinks, hand in hand, like lovers . . .

'There's a coffin going down Fhearchar's croft, and one at the end of ours,' said her mother.

'*Three of theirs and one of mine*,' said the ghost of Mairi an Seer.

The Wishing Well

Walking into the night with the great wild range of the Cuillins looming ahead of her, looking sometimes near and sometimes far, like great monsters in a dream; in such surroundings the insult seemed a small thing, diminished and unimportant, but then she had already walked some seven or eight miles, long enough to simmer down, and was well on the way to Sligachan. She could easily stay at the hotel there; she didn't need to have any money (as indeed she hadn't). She had left the dance hall as she stood, in a midnight-blue evening gown and swathed in a mohair stole, chin high, nose in air; no one could insult her, no one could say as Torquil had done – that he hoped she would remain a spinster for the rest of her mortal days. He said she was a rolling stone and could never go for long enough with the one fellow to give him a chance to propose to her. Well, all right, let him find her now, let him search the whole of Skye for her, and good luck to him!

There was still a half light. She slackened her pace a bit as her indignation cooled off and became aware of the fact that her shoes were most inadequate. Should she break the high heels off? She had seen tinker girls walking for miles behind their carts, in wedding slippers. If they could stick it, why shouldn't she? After all, if she were accosted by a wild heifer, a stag or even that daddy of them all the Water Kelpie, she could defend herself with them.

Heading down into a valley now, the mist entirely enveloping her, she could see nothing and felt deadly cold. Her dress was clinging to her damp and chill. Then slowly the grass began to show green again at the sides of the road as she ploughed her way up into the open. What would she say to them when she did reach Sligachan? Granted they were relations, but what would they think of her, stravaiging along a deserted road at dead of night in a chiffon dress and slippers . . . and yet if she kept on past the hotel, it would be lunchtime tomorrow before she could possibly reach home . . . a good thirty miles . . . surely they would catch up with her before then? Even if Torquil didn't come, surely her cousins would. She imagined the car brakes screeching behind her and Torquil leaping out, beseeching her to forgive him, telling her that he never meant to offend her. Then it suddenly occurred to her that they might not guess that she had attempted to walk home. Why the heck should they? Maybe they were still looking for her in Portree.

Well, it was too late to turn back now, and even if they came this very minute she doubted very much if she would accept a lift . . . that is, not for at least another half mile. Besides, this was an experience, an adventure, it could never happen again. She could tell her children about it, sitting snugly by the fire, with Torquil puffing away at his pipe. *Him* – why she wouldn't marry him for all the tea in China – and she half ran, half stumbled down another hill to rid herself of such a thought. At the bottom it was dark again, a valley filled with shadows looming up all round like giant dancing partners, a *danse macabre*. She halted, rigid with fear, till suddenly the clouds fell away from the summit Sgurr Alasdair and a great hole of light came in the sky . . . somewhere it was morning. She had a ghastly feeling that in the mist and darkness she had drifted onto the Mol, or coast road, instead of going over the newly re-opened Drumuie Brae . . . could she have bypassed Sligachan? . . . she was desolate . . . no cars would find her now.

She began to realise that she had just finished being very frightened indeed, so she began to cry – and then to laugh – for there, through the first rays of morning sun she could make out the sharp silver thread of the Sligachan River making its way to the sea.

This meant that she had been walking all through the night. Now that she could see clearly in the early morning sunlight there were no longer any ghosts, so she took off her worn-through slippers and shoved her stockings inside them. The cool, short grass at the edge of the road was heaven for her feet, for a while at any rate.

When she reached the river she dipped her blistered feet into the ice cold water, and listened to the rumbling of her tummy and the gurgling of the river harmonising perfectly, and knew that if she didn't eat something soon, it would be a corpse they would find on the road. The very idea filled her with self-pity. Would Torquil feel it was his fault? Would he go to the funeral? Would they bury her at Aiseag, where the rabbits eat into the graves, or at Cill Chriosd where the bereaved coffin bearers scatter their empty whisky bottles? Pity, she thought, never to have written a will. She would have requested to be buried at sea; you go down three times before you actually sink, which gives you a chance to change your mind . . . then how could you change your mind if you were already dead? Dead! I'm not dead yet . . . I'm only sixteen. I'm just bloody hungry. They say if you drink plenty of water you don't feel quite so desperate. It was dangerous to drink from the rivers, though. Then she remembered the well; it was a wishing well similar to the one at Aiseag. She had passed it once in the car, about a year ago. It was built low at the side of the road with a sort of stone roof on it, like a chapel . . . a sort of confessional. Every human soul needs something like that. Take the priests, and today the psychiatrists, and shouting up the chimney at Christmas. Oh, yes, but you have to pay for a wish, she had forgotten that.

As she approached the well she looked around for something to give. She suddenly saw a clump of Lady's Slipper growing round the well, little yellow mossy flowers all clumped together . . . you see, Lady's Slipper – why, she would leave hers – they were hurting her again anyway. She placed them neatly on a stone at the side of the well, and wished so ardently that she nearly fell in . . . Did the spirits of the wishing well not appreciate her gift? She had always understood that they were rather partial to shoes and boots. After all, they had very little opportunity of seeing much else.

There was a man she once heard of in Achaidh a'Chumhaing,* and the spirits warned him that if he were caught outside with his boots undone harm would befall him. Well, he defied them, and fell to his neck in a dung-heap.

As she knelt there, cupping her hands and preparing to drink, the heat of the sun now burning through her chiffon dress, she began to be afraid again – afraid she might swallow a tadpole. She had heard of a man once who had swallowed

* Achaidh a'Chumhaing – Field of the Strait

one, and it turned into a frog. It hopped about so much inside him that he had to keep hopping with it (the timing was perfect) . . . Then, she didn't believe all that people said. Her grandmother told her that if she killed a toad it would croak in her ear for ever. Cartagena from the village (no one knows her right name) says that if you lock a person suffering from worms in a closed dark barn, and make him breathe from a barrel filled with dead frogs, the stench will make him vomit his guts out, and so he will be cured. (Sometimes it fails, though, she says.) Cartagena was good at telling stories, although one could never be quite sure if they were true.

There was the one about the young man who strangled his sweetheart. Every day, when he went to draw water from the well, the white marguerites and wild narcissi round about got splashed with blood instead of water, before his very eyes, so much so that he had to flee the country. If you cross the ocean things like that stop . . . but no one ever saw him again to tell whether it did, or not.

Taking another look at the Sligachan Hotel through half-closed eyes smarting from sunlight and exposure, she realised that it was not so near as she had at first thought. Raising herself up from the side of the well, having drunk herself full, she moved to a clump of thistles. She knew, perhaps instinctively, that there is a sort of cheese-like stuff inside a thistlehead. It's a knowledge that starts before memory begins, before one is born . . . taking a grip of life, the first struggle – the first necessity – food. Getting two stones she banged the bristles off them, and sure enough, there was food, little lumps of solid cheese. As she ate she began to get more sleepy, and half-dreamt, half-thought about wells in general, and the cave she had once heard of on the Island of Rona, with a font in it.

On the shining rock behind the dripping font the wet walls gleamed and shone, and the figure of the Virgin Mary could be clearly seen. They saw that figure on Rona long before Bernadette saw hers at Lourdes . . . Lourdes . . . Oh! Holy Mary, help me, let someone find me, I am so tired . . . The spirits of the wells aren't working for me, and anyway why should they? They have been ignored for too long, they are offended by the inflated pneumatic tyres of cars and tractors, instead of the warm patter of human feet. Yes, that was it – the spirits of the wells are afraid – could you blame them? Think of Tobar Aiseig, that ancient well down by the graveyard; now that they talk of building an airstrip there, soon the smooth green grassland at the edge of the sea would be scattered with aeroplanes, not cows chewing away contentedly. You could not go there to ask for a lid full of warm foaming milk straight from the udder. Imagine, in a holy place like that – where the Columban monks and Saint Maolrubha himself used to ring a bell on a holly tree, or was it a Holy tree – to summon the folks to worship. It was enough to make all the corpses in the graveyard rise up in protest. There would be no more mushrooms either, growing on the short smooth sea grass. No more helping to tie the legs of frisking cows, nor could you dance on the gleaming white sands to the tunes of the melodeon; and worst of all, what would be the use of wishing at a wishing well if it was soon to be turned into a ladies' powder room, or a ticket office where you could buy a return ticket to Glasgow, or, perhaps New York? I won't think about that, it's too horrible, not at all what wishing wells are for. Wishing wells must be for exhausted travellers like me. Wishing and wishing and wishing for someone to come . . .

Gradually her limbs became limp and relaxed as she leant against the small green hillock that protected and hid the well. She painfully struggled to keep awake (like in church). It must be getting late. She shivered a bit. She simply must move herself, make an effort. No, it was no use. She became aware of sheep appearing from nowhere. Gradually they nibbled their way nearer and nearer to where she was sitting; she could feel their warmth already. She had heard of this before, how the sheep clustered round lost children, to keep them warm, but she never dreamt it could happen to her.

The light was slowly going, and the sun was setting. It must be late afternoon. Soon all she could see was the warm mass of sheep's backsides encircling her, and she fell fast asleep.

She must have slept for many hours and woke up in terror, cold sweat pouring off her. The sheep had all gone. She thought she heard dogs barking and men's voices shouting her name . . . could it be a nightmare? Everything was pitch dark, except for what looked like torches bearing down on her through the night. Then to her utmost relief and joy she recognised the enormous girth of her favourite aunt carrying a length of rope and a shepherd's crook.

'The whole island's been looking for you, my girl. Are you all right? What happened?' she asked as she unscrewed the top of a brandy flask. 'Drink that up, and don't breathe a word to a living soul!'

Sure enough, there had been a general alert, 'missing girl' and all that; a search party was formed . . . and there they all were, shepherds and dogs, climbing guides and gillies, hotel porters and tourists, to say nothing of Big Archie, the policeman from Portree.

What could she say? How could she tell them all that . . . that Torquil had insulted her? It sounded so silly. Where was he, anyway? 'Torquil . . . where's Torquil? Oh! There you are.'

He was rubbing her bare blistered feet between his hands. They were completely numb, and she hadn't felt a thing. As she stretched both her arms towards him, she whispered, 'Can you forgive me, darling?'

'No!' he shouted in a loud voice, 'but maybe I'll buy you a new pair of slippers . . . since you went and lost your own.'

Consider an Island

If you think of an island in the middle of the sea, well, that's where islands usually are, it's green and sunny at the south end and things grow well. At the north end it's rugged, mountainous, with whispering purple grey mist caressing it. But you can come down from the clouds for a moment, I want to tell you about my people as they really were a century ago.*

Picture a hand-made house, made of hand-hewn rock with walls eighteen inches thick, and thatched with hand-plucked reed, secured with straw ropes, big stones dangling on the ends of them to hold fishing nets in place; and usually there would be a line of salt fish hung on an iron wedge in the wall. And there was always a stack of peat at the end of the house which served also as a men's convenience during the wet weather.

During the fine weather this particular chap I want to tell you about, he was rather odd, would take a large quantity of books outside to the end of the house where the sun was, then shout to his wife to bring him a chair – two magnificent slabs of shiny, thick wood supported by four splay-footed stumps of branches. She brought it of course immediately, being only a woman. She didn't want to be clobbered.

* This story is absolutely true.

Women did all the work in those days. 'Fetch the water, milk the cow, feed the hens, cart the peat, pull the plough.' It just left you enough time to bear the children and bake the bannocks, and, let's face it, things haven't changed much.

It's the eighteenth century and Big Donald Angus Macleod, scholar, bard, a sort of high priest of the community, is sitting at the side of his house with his top hat on – because he had one! They didn't all have toppers, only the doctor, the minister and himself. The visiting schoolmaster didn't have one always, it made his head sweat when he had all those miles to walk from village to village; and the boys would be sure to sit on it half hidden in the straw on the mud floor, there were no seats in the bochans of barns used as schoolrooms in those days. But once the schoolmaster had left his hat behind. And the following month, when he'd remembered where he had laid it down, there was a litter of ginger and white striped kittens in it. He was too soft-hearted to shift them.

Big Donald Angus used to say that the schoolmaster was too soft-hearted altogether; his predecessor had thrashed the scholars that couldn't learn 'Man's Chief End' or Chaucer and Virgil before they were twelve. He did it so: he got a cauldron and spilt half a bottle of burgundy into it, and some boiling water, not too much as he would be drinking the stuff himself afterwards, to get his strength back. Then he'd add a couple of cloves and take the tawse down from the hook on the wall. It is a long narrow strip of leather. He would then cut five fingers at the end of it, with the knife he used for cutting up the black twist and nipping the ears of the sheep. He would then boil the strap in the burgundy for twenty minutes, and bend the offending little amadan over his knee and see how many strokes he could give him before exhausting himself completely. 'Yes, that's the way it was in my day,' Donald Angus would say. Now don't run away with the idea that Big Donald Angus was a tyrant, quite the reverse! He was too lazy to come in out of the rain.

'It's starting to rain, Angus,' his wife would call to him, 'and the hens are cackling all over your new books. Oh, dear me, you'll be the death of me!'

'Get ye to a nunnery, woman!' he'd quote from a tattered book of *Hamlet*, and he would continue to read.

'Where is it, Angus?' she'd say, tossing her youngest to her left breast for a change and kicking the twins back into the house with her bare feet. But he couldn't be bothered explaining Shakespeare to her, she was only his wife.

His oldest daughter, Cairistiona, was quite a different kettle of fish. Besides, she was easy on the eye, not like the old bag Rebecca, his wife. Mind you, she too had been a bit of a humdinger in her day . . . he had had an awful job getting her, in fact. She was of good family you see; instead of her bringing him a dowry of six or seven head of cattle, he'd had to go and fight for her – capture her and bring her away – for nothing. She had lived on a smaller island some miles off and was already bespoken of by her cousin, who was a handsome young laird. So naturally she was preparing a very fine dowry working night and day at her spinning wheel.

Then one dark night while out netting the mouth of his rival's river, Big Donald Angus suddenly thought it would be a good idea or ploy to sail right close up to the island and help himself to the lot. The cattle. Well, the calves would have to do. He only had a forty-two-foot boat and nine men, but he could manage to take the hens and bed and bedding all right, and the dowry chest and of course not forgetting the desirable Rebecca herself. Oh, and the spinning wheel!

It was an enterprising venture requiring guerrilla-like strategies, especially when they sighted the young laird's boat coming round the headland straight for them. He had a bigger boat than them, mind you, and twenty men at his disposal. The battle that ensued was worse than the Armada itself. What a stramash! Servants, cattle, hens and furniture were all floating about on the tide. Big Donald Angus grabbed ahold of Rebecca by the feet and slung her over his shoulder; he managed to shove a young piglet under his oxter at the same time, and one of his men got the spinning wheel. It was all they could do in the circumstances because they were well outnumbered, after all.

Now the funny thing is, Rebecca wouldn't speak to him after that for a long, long time, not until after three of their children were born in fact. He began to think she was dumb. Then one day she found her own old spinning wheel up in the loft and thinking herself alone, she began to sing. Big Donald Angus heard her and was delighted. There were seven more children born after that.

And as I was just about to tell you, the oldest one was called Cairistiona, and not only was she beautiful, she was damned clever, too, so the schoolmaster said (he had a notion for her). Instead of falling asleep in the hay on the classroom floor like most of his other pupils, she actually learnt how to speak English, not only just read and write it, but speak it. Big Donald Angus said she was the only one of his ten children that took after him. She would sometimes sit with him in the sun at the side of the house, laughing her head off over Dante's *Visions of Hell* or (as the story came to be handed down) the Crofters' Reform Bill. They had a lot in common.

Donald Angus felt he would be reluctant to part with her. It was nevertheless clear that she was ripening, and that Torquil the laird's son was beginning to have an eye for her. Well, Big Donald didn't want that, even if it did mean a couple of stirks as compensation. Lifting her at the jigging in the barn was all right occasionally, and the young pup could fairly whisk her off her feet, but Big Donald thought the schoolmaster would be a far better proposition. He had felt quite sorry for the poor fella as he stood at the door nibbling his nails to the quick with nervous frustration. He would be quite an asset as a son-in-law, with all those books of his. But as yet Cairistiona didn't seem to think much of either of them. She was still half wild and spent most of her time with Voltaire her brother (called Wally for short) down at the nearby harbour, chatting up the fisher girls at the gutting or watching the foreign ships loading cargo.

That's how they came to hear the rumours that were going about. At that time many fishing boats came into the harbour, mostly for shelter, sometimes as many as fifty, all nationalities, and the women could get work there gutting the herring. It was poorly paid certainly, but how could they dispute that since they couldn't speak Russian, French, Danish or even English, and they were far too shy. Anyway, the fish dealers and the excise men would never listen to them.

So it is not surprising that one of the local fishermen set himself as a sort of go-between. He had acquired a smattering of many languages on his travels, and was bitter and greedy through having been chain-ganged in his youth. He set himself up as a sort of universal aunt, an agent or employment bureau; he negotiated with a man from a far distant place called Manchester; the girls were offered wonderful jobs if they would go there, highly paid, as much as ten shillings a week I think it was, to work in the cotton mills. And many of them went.

Now the odd thing was there was no word from them after they left home. The agent said they were enjoying life fine and liking the work, but there was not a word from the girls themselves, and the parents were getting worried. After all, this Manchester was a foreign land about which they knew nothing. And there were all sorts of rumours going about. Some said that Tormod Cameron the agent and some of the Russians off the boats were trying out an experiment on one of the small islands and they needed the girls for it. It was called a nu . . . nu-dist camp, or something like that. They said they were all running around naked and playing tig to keep themselves warm, but no one really believed a word of it. So that's why they came to Big Donald Angus for advice.

They didn't come empty-handed either; even Perry Mason has his price. They brought that cask of whisky that got washed ashore last week in the storm – it was a mystery where it came from – and Cairistiona and her brother Voltaire plucked half a dozen chickens and cooked them on the swee, or slabhraidh, above the peat fire. 'It's no good trying to make a plan on an empty stomach,' Big Donald always said, and this is what he decided should be done.

Cairistiona would go to the agent and ask him for a job.

She would not let on she understood any English and would listen to every word, every word mind you, that was said between the agent and the officers of the ships. The schoolmaster and Voltaire would follow her to see that she came to no harm. 'Let me know if you hear anything fishy,' Big Donald Angus had said, and sent her off to make a start by gutting the herring amongst the other girls.

Sure enough, Tormod the agent was not long in spotting her. He had a good nose for the women, and this one was surely the pick of them all. He sat on an upturned barrel and tossed a couple of sovereigns from one greasy palm to the other. He asked her in the Gaelic if she would like to earn a decent wage working in the cotton mills in Manchester, instead of spluttering around in fish gut? She said she would. So he said he would go straightaway and fix accommodation for her on one of the ships. There were nine other girls going too, and they would leave for a place called Liverpool the following day, weather permitting and God willing. The old hypocrite! After about twenty minutes he came back again accompanied by two other men. They were very fat and had gold in their teeth and their beards were black and bushy like eagles' nests, and they looked at her as though she were a heifer, assessing the girth, height and weight of her. She felt they could see right through her semmit and began to blush.

Then they started talking rapidly to Tormod in English. That was a piece of luck, and she understood every word. It seems they were bargaining, they were offering him seven pounds, for her. It seemed like a lot of money. They said they'd make it ten if he found them another girl like this one. Tormod said it wasn't enough, and they told him they couldn't pay more as they would have a great deal more expense with this lot than with the last lot they had taken. The depot in Manchester had been closed down since then by the police, so these girls would have to be shipped from Liverpool to South America direct.

South America . . . in the name of the wee man,* what would her father say when she told him this! Promising the agent she would be back first thing in the morning with her belongings, she rejoined her brother and the schoolmaster and they beat it back home as fast as their legs would carry them.

And when they told Big Donald Angus what she'd heard he got the whole clan together, and with villagers from far and near carrying ropes and knives and torches, they all marched down to the harbour at dead of night. They boarded the ship bound for Liverpool and cut the rigging and flooded the bilges and tore down the sails. Then they gagged and roped the captain, the agent, the crew, the white-slave traffickers. They just took the lot and made a big pile of them on the pier; then flung them into carts and gigs and wheelbarrows and trundled them off to be dealt with by the fiscal himself; who pointed out (wisely enough) that a little knowledge of English language (ugly an' all as it was) could be a very useful thing at times!

Oh! I forgot to tell you: Cairistiona and the schoolmaster started building a house with eighteen-inch thick walls, and

---

* . . . in the name of the wee man – an ainm an duine bhig. It's just like saying 'for heaven's sake', or 'my goodness'. The 'wee man' could be in the days of fairies or in the days of angels . . . And could have been one of the early Skye monks, Saint Maolrubha of Aiseag.

a small distillery under the floor. And needless to say, the wedding they had lasted right through the winter, which was wet anyway – and they had two children – just imagine that! Would you believe it?*

---

* According to my mother Marianna Macleod's diary, Big Donald Angus, or Duncan Bán as he was known, would be my great-great-grandfather. From her letter (1954): 'Rhona wanted me to write the names of our ancestors. My father was Angus Macleod, son of Neil, son of Duncan Bàn, son of Allan, son of Murdo. My mother was Rebecca Mackinnon, daughter of Donald Mackinnon and Cairistiona Finlayson. We are supposed to be of the Raasay Macleods.'

Father on the Island

It was the late end of the year and my father had got permission to shoot on one of the small islands. So he called Iain Mór the keeper and Seonaidh Ceitidh the poacher into the dining room for a conference, which meant a large dram. 'We'll take the dinghy and row out to the island and the sooner the better. Here, fill your pockets with these.' He handed out some bottles. 'Right then, off we . . . what do you want, girl?'

I'd thrown my small body against the girth of my father as he left the room. 'Please, please, take me with you . . .'

'You know there's only room for three in the dinghy. You're not old enough . . . oh, all right. Oilskins, gumboots, the lot mind you – and you are not to land, understand? You won't move from the dinghy all the time we are away, and it will be a devil of a long time I can assure you!'

It took about twenty minutes for the men to row out to the little sandy beach on Guillamon, then they clambered ashore, leaving me most unhappily in charge of the boat. I watched forlornly their bulky bodies moving up the face of the cliff, climbing all the time and getting more distant like flies moving round a lampshade – soon they would be out of sight. I wished I was a boy; my cousin was allowed to carry a gun at twelve. I was thirteen-and-a-half. I stripped off and had a swim, then popped the buds on seaweed and sulked until it got cold. I heard a few shots on the far side of the island. I began to hate men. I would tell my mother how much whisky they had with them. Then I remembered there was a shinty match tonight in Carbost. I must get back. It was getting dusk. I loathed my father now.

I decided to take the boat and leave them. I seized the oars and shoved them in the rowlocks. I threw my weight against the boat and launched her. I climbed in, drenched myself to the thighs in my enthusiasm, and rowed. Eventually I reached the shore and made fast to a big boulder and started to run for home. I slackened pace and slowed down, then a great surge of guilt came over me. I stopped dead and realised I couldn't go home and tell my mother I had left Father on an uninhabited island with no boat, no means of getting off – and he couldn't live on whisky, or could he? I saw a tinker's tent – they were all right, I knew them . . .

I sat on a couple of peats and took a cigarette which I rolled for myself. I didn't like their tea, it was too strong. 'What will I do?' I asked. They were very silent.

The old man thought, 'Go home, girl. Your father will see the steamer going into Kyle of Lochalsh in the morning. She goes pretty close to Guillamon. If he fires a few shots they may see him.'

Small comfort. As I got to the front steps of our house I felt sick. I dare not go in. I hadn't the courage. So I crept round the back and threw clods of earth at Té Bhearnas-dail's* bedroom window. Té Bhearnasdail was a maid we had who was supposed to be simple. I thought her very clever. She came down and I got her advice.

* Té Bhearnasdail – the woman from Bernisdale

'It's all very well for your father and mother,' she said, 'but what about Iain Mór's wife and Seonaidh Ceitidh's parrot?'

'We'll forget the parrot, but you'd better run over and see Iain Mór's wife.'

Té Bhearnasdail lumbered over the dyke and ran across the field to Iain Mór's – she came back at the double. 'Iain Mór's wife,' she said in the Gaelic, 'is down on her knees in the middle of the kitchen in the lamplight praying for her husband's return. There's only one thing for you to do: take my bike and cycle all the way to Kyleakin, stay with your aunt there and tell her you have to go to the mainland to get a tooth out without delay. I'll throw your clothes out of the window, and plead ignorance for the rest of my mortal days!'

As for those three men, they deserved all they got, and so said the skipper of the fishing boat that picked them up next morning . . . And funnily enough, so said Mother.

Septimus

To be the seventh son of a seventh son means that you more than likely have been born with a certain kind of magic, a creative sort of magic. And this gift is never ignored by the folk of any Highland village.

So it was then, that when Curstag Bhàn was about to deliver her seventh child, all the cailleachs in the village congregated round to give her a helping hand; they were scuttling round her like hens on a hot girdle and so taken up with delivering the baby that they didn't realise, the poor mother was gravely ill. In fact, she died a few hours after her child was born. And Big Iain her husband was beside himself with rage and grief. He could no longer stand the house without his wife and helpmate, and he was at his wits' end what on earth to do with all those seven children.

Well, it so happened there was a lady missionary staying for a short holiday up at the hotel, and when she heard of the poor man's plight, him being left with all this brood of orphans, she took pity on him and like any striving Christian asked if there was anything she could do to help.

'Nothing that I can see,' said Big Iain, 'unless you want to take over where my wife left off?'

'Marry you, do you mean?' said the missionary, unable to believe her luck.

'Just so,' said Iain, but he didn't believe she would take him up on it, her being a lady of quality and all that.

Well, she took him up on it all right, no sooner said than done. She was a born organiser and wasted no time at all in finding homes for the six elder children with relatives in Edinburgh. The baby she just left with a wet-nurse in the village, then carted poor Iain off to Nigeria to help her convert the heathen.

That was all very commendable, but after a year or more it so happened that the wet-nurse died, leaving the baby barely weaned, and the local minister could not find any trace of Iain or his new bride in Africa or Edinburgh or anywhere. So the wee Septimus was left to the mercy of the villagers who kept him and fed him as best they could, taking turns of mending and caring for him. They also came to love him very dearly, especially when they discovered that he had a great gift for music. He could play the chanter before he was five and he began to make all kinds of instruments for himself, and play tunes on them, tunes he got from the birds, from the singing burns and the wind in the trees. You could hear him imitating birds and getting the sounds of mosquitoes even out of a paper and comb.

The villagers were so impressed by his talent that they got the minister to speak to the local laird on his behalf. But the local laird, although he was a very rich and influential man, had very little interest in the lives and needs of his tenants. So the gifted little lad had to learn to fend for himself, and as time went on it became the top of his ambition to make for himself a violin, a beautiful shining violin. He worked in the fields to earn the money to buy the wood and waxes that he would need – and in his enthusiasm he forgot all about the needs of his body.

So by the time he was fifteen he was in decline, and the sound of his music weakened till it was but a whisper in the wind. So it was then that the seventh son of a seventh son was buried down by the river and a little cairn of white stones put to his head.

Meanwhile, the laird, a cultured and music-loving man, was taking a holiday in Milan, and there he chanced to hear the sweet music of a little Italian called Guiseppi, a little unknown bastard, completely forlorn. He was so impressed that he took the boy under his wing, bought him fine clothes and a violin that cost the earth, poshed him up with proper manners and started bragging of him as his protégé; he even brought him back home with him. It was then that the strange thing happened.

Almost as soon as he arrived at the village Guiseppi felt a strange urge to walk along by the river. Suddenly, he felt tired and sat for a while by a little cairn of white stones. As he sat there he became inspired and he thought he could hear strange sweet music all around him. So, reaching for his new violin which never left his side, he tucked it under his chin and tuned it thoughtfully, then dissolved into a sort of trance as though he were half dead. His fingers alone were alive, frenzied one moment, then gentle and caressing; he had never played like this before. It was divine, slowly the salt tears ran down his small dark face . . . he could taste them now with the corner of his mouth. He was coming alive again, the perspiration oozing from his brow and the call of the birds coming from under his bow, the whistle of the wind and the buzzing of bees. This was reincarnation, the unveiling of a ghost of music that Guiseppi knew he never could himself have composed.

He was surrounded by villagers when he came to himself again, villagers with damp smouldering eyes, choked with emotion, who seemed as though they had a question to ask him but didn't quite know how, for the music they heard they knew . . . full well . . . but the lad they had never seen before.

Chains

Iain Beag was worried about the storm outside. It made him think about the boat and wonder if he had beached her high enough. Would the rope hold to the boulder he had chosen? So he said to his brother Iain Mór, 'Go out and take a look at the boat.'

'Go yourself,' said Iain Mór.

'Man, I can't. Can't you see I'm in the middle of doing my homework? Ach, all right then, leisgeadair bochd.'* And Iain Beag reached for his sou'wester and slammed the door behind him. When he reached down the croft his anxiety fell away from him, for the boat was high and dry up on the machair, but he could hear the barn door groaning and moaning on its hinges. So he continued on down to the shore to find something to fix it with.

He and his brother were twins and they relied almost entirely on what they could find on the shore, since they were orphans and very poor. Their father, who had been drowned at sea, left them only the croft and the boat, and their mother had died when they were born. The people round about were good to them, and their very good friend the priest had given them a new suit of clothes on their thirteenth birthday; and when they wore the jackets they would turn them inside out

* leisgeadair bochd – lazy wretch

or sit back to back, to save rubbing against the rough stone kitchen walls of their home. They were good lads both of them and were doing well at the school.

Well, when Iain Beag was down at the shore that wild night looking round for something to fix the barn door with, he heard a sinister sort of rattling that seemed to be coming from the surface of the water. It was getting nearer and there was a rhythmic music with it, a sort of holy chant, swishing and murmuring . . . 'one two, one two' . . . almost like rowing. Just then a huge wave landed at his feet – carrying a great heavy length of chain with a large wide loop at the end of it. The very thing for the barn door, thought Iain as he lumbered it up the croft.

In the night the storm abated, although Iain hadn't slept a wink for thinking of the tune he had heard, he kept trying to put words to the persistent monotonous beat. It was like counting sheep and he didn't fall asleep till it was time to get up again.

Later that morning he and his brother put their jackets on, the right way round for it was Sunday. Iain Beag didn't bother walking back with his brother from the church, for the stupid glaoich had gone and got himself a click. So he would have to go back home on his own, but first he thought he knew where there was a plover's nest. The eggs were good eating and would do for their dinner.

It was an easy climb down the face of the rock, but Iain had forgotten to take off his jacket. He felt cumbersome and awkward and when the front of it stuck on a jutting out branch the buttons gave way, and before he could take a better grip he was falling and falling down to the sea below. . . . When he regained consciousness he felt himself being

74

carried to the shingle in the arms of a completely strange man. He was very brown and his massive body was bare to the waist.

'Who are you, sir?' said Iain, 'I would like to thank you.'

'Don't-a thank me-a,' said the man in a foreign accent, 'it is I who must thank you for liberating my soul.' And slowly the man's body seemed to move backwards into the sea again and his voice became distant like the strange music . . . chanting in Latin, '*Galierus servus sum . . . Galierus servus sum . . .*' or had he heard that in the church? He couldn't be sure any more . . . maybe it was just concussion.

The brothers did well all that year at the school. And as a man Iain Beag did even better than his brother; he got himself a bursary for Edinburgh University and managed to take honours in History and Languages. The old priest had helped him a lot, of course, and they were still close friends. In fact, it was he who had told Iain the legend or story of the galleon that had been washed up on these shores many years ago and of the slaves who had been drowned in it, unable to release themselves from their chains.

'*They say you can still hear their cries on a wild night, chanting over the waters like a Latin Mass.*'

'Maybe not now,' thought Iain, 'not all of them, that is.' For the chain of one of them he felt quite sure was hanging on his own barn door.

Mare's Tail

Many years ago there was a priest living on one of the Outer Hebridean Islands. 'An Sagart' he was called in the Gaelic, and his flock adored him, partly because he could be like any ordinary man; he had the same interests as themselves, he liked his food and his wine and he loved horses and was not above having a wee flutter at the races.

Now, some ponies had been shipped recently to a flat green island ideal for breaking them in, and the Sagart used to get a boy to row him over to the island, to 'study form', so to speak. They were a clumsy, heavy-looking lot of beasts when they were first brought over from Ireland, but a week or so after they were put on the little green isle they started to mysteriously acquire much more graceful movements; they looked different and no one could understand why. It was nothing to do with the trainer who was breaking them in, he was just an ordinary coarse sort of chap who couldn't have achieved such miraculous results in the time.

So the Priest, holy man and all as he was, had to agree that there was something phenomenal about it. So he decided one night to row out on his own when there was no one about, to study their movements in peace and quiet. It was at the time of the full moon, and the young horses silhouetted black against the skyline were a sight for sore eyes. The Sagart took the boat close in to where there was a little shingle, a mixture of white sand and shells, the clear water rippling over it like champagne. He shipped his oars and settled his back against the gunwales in the prow of the boat, and set himself to watch.

There was not a murmur in the wind and the horses were passive, some stretched out on the ground, and some standing in their sleep the way horses do. You could see the warm dew rising from the grass, turned silver in the night, and now and then an odd stamping or snorting was all that split the silence . . . When, suddenly, there was a sound like disturbed waters . . . a sort of 'ploop' like a porpoise or a seal might make . . . and onto the sky-line at the far side of the island an apparition arose . . . a thing, the like of which he had never before seen or heard of. It rose out of the water, dispersing white spray like a fountain all around it, and soared up into the sky . . . then landed through the silver mist down amongst the ponies.

It was a Green Horse, a Mare of such exquisite beauty it was spellbinding, its colour was pale green, a sort of translucent green like Chinese jade (or Orcadian waters), its tail was long and white like chiffon and its mane was also white, and the antics of it were astonishing. It preened and tishied around on golden hoofs, rising in the air on its hind legs like a ballet dancer. And the extraordinary thing was that the ponies all did likewise; they followed her every move and copied her every gesture, they were completely transformed. It was easy to see now where they were getting their training from . . . this Green Mare was hynotising them. They danced and danced in the moonlight and never ceased till dawn . . . when gradually a halo of morning light began to shine on the Green Mare . . . dissolving her . . . she evaporated, till there was nothing left but a streaky cloud known to mariners as 'the Mare's Tail', and the only sound you could hear was the 'ploop' that she made as she returned once more through the rippling water.

The Sagart gripped the oars in numb hands and replaced them with difficulty back in the rowlocks. He listened to the swish and monophonic rhythm of the oars bringing him back home and to reality. He would never go there again; he had heard, of course of pink elephants, but never before of green horses.*

* You know when you see a Mare's Tail that it's going to rain. That is common knowledge. But this story was inspired by an occasion when Macdonald of Tote (on the north end of Skye near Skeabost) decided to experiment with putting some horses on the Island of Pabay. He had a huge boat (I don't know where they got it from, it must have been a very ancient one and very strong) and put two horses at a time into the boat, trying to get them rowed across. But of course they only went a few yards out from shore when the horses jumped ship and decided to swim back, and some of them landed up in Elgol and some in nearer places like Dunan and Luib, and the whole enterprise was a total failure. Macdonald was a very fine man, very eccentric, much respected and much talked about. He dressed magnificently, the kilt of course. And knowing and respecting and liking this man very much I conceived this ridiculous story.

The Helik Stag

There was a gemmer once living on a small mountainous island off Skye, Scalpay I think it was. Anyway, there were lots of stags on it. In the late end of the year you could see their antlers silhouetted against the glowing colours of the Northern Lights. It was a beautiful sight.

Now this gemmer was a very conscientious sort of fellow, and it was his habit to walk right round the island every single day no matter what the weather was like. Well, this day he was kind of pressed for time as he had promised to play the melodeon at a dance over in Skye. They were counting on him; if he didn't go they would be stuck. So he decided to take a shorter route this time; instead of keeping round by the shore he would make his way through the hills.

He was climbing away, his head bent down looking at his feet, a thing you should never do for any length of time . . . when suddenly ahead of him he saw a big white stag, a seventeen-pointer, a regular beauty. He had never seen a beast like it before and was sure it wasna canny.* He was glad his old gun was iron. It was no good trying to shoot at a spook, the shot would skyte right through him and leave him standing fresh as ever. But if you touched them with iron they vanished, so it was said.

* wasna canny – unnatural

So he started to stalk it, crawling on his belly and keeping down wind. He pursued it out of curiosity more than an intent to kill (he was a brave man). It led him by stops and starts right up to where there was a black-looking loch all covered in magic swirling mist that made a hissing noise like steam, and the wings of dragonflies sparkled in it, and there, into the black waters the white stag completely disappeared. The hissing mist had suddenly cleared and the surface of the water was undisturbed. There was nothing save the sound of the dragonflies singing. In a state of confusion he arrived home and told the yarn as best he could – even his mother wouldn't believe him.

Some weeks later they heard that a young lad had gone missing, a stranger he was, hiking his way through the Islands. He was very blond and spoke with a foreign accent. The local policeman had been alerted and all gemmers and gillies were told to watch out for any sign of him. So when the Scalpay gemmer got to thinking the matter out, it suddenly struck him to try the spooky loch again.

So he led a party of willing stalwarts up the mountain path towards the loch and, sure enough, they lifted the stranger's body out from its depths. . . . A white stag is not often seen in this country, but in foreign lands it's a well known holy messenger with the Cross on its brow.*

---

* 'Hubert was very fond of hunting and one Good Friday went out after a stag when everybody else was going to church. In a clearing of the wood the beast turned, displaying a crucifix between its horns. Hubert stopped in astonishment, and a voice came from the stag, saying, "Unless you turn to the Lord, Hubert, you shall fall into Hell." St Hubert is patron saint of hunting-men, and is invoked against hydrophobia.' (from Butler's *Lives of the Saints*)

Flight of Fancy

Rain was beating on the glass roof of the dilapidated work-shop where we kept our boat. The birds that nested in the holes and grooves of the crumbling stone wall were well camouflaged by cobwebs and piles of old sacks. About fifty years ago the place had been a carpenter's shop, and there was still a lot of sawdust and shavings piled up behind the bench; the birds could line their nests with it, and the mice could hide in it and we of course were adding daily to the pile up with our sawing, sanding and scraping.

The boat had been an open thirty-two-foot launch, and we were trying to convert her, struggling to build a cabin and wheelhouse and at the same time taking care not to make her too top-heavy as (a) we wouldn't be able to get her out of the workshop, and (b) she would probably capsize when we got her onto the water (if we ever succeeded in getting her onto the water, that is). We were suffering from acute depression at the time. Then we bought the boat Kazik (my husband) had been working on as a design engineer, till one day the centrifugal experiment he was trying out blew up and he landed in hospital. When he got out and was ready to resume work he found the firm was no more, it had gone bust. Finances consequently were very low. We paid weekly for the use of this workshop, and had recently been given an ultimatum: we must get out, they needed the space, the old building would be pulled down and new premises built in its place . . . We could no longer be accommodated . . . nor the birds . . . nor the mice.

So we used the remainder of our money to buy wood, brass screws, copper nails and glue, to say nothing of paint; and worked nonstop to get the work finished. I was busy sanding a piece of wood to make a table in the galley. It had been the lid of my mother's sewing table, for all our spare furniture was going into this boat – two wardrobes, my father's piano stool and all the bed ends we could find. We even had a mahogany lavatory seat as a facing to a cubby-hole or locker. I had a lump in my throat and tears kept welling as I scraped at the sewing table lid . . . my mother had adored it so much. I kept thinking about her as I rounded the edges with a Stanley file. She had been born and brought up in the Isle of Skye and had had nine brothers and one sister. Most of her brothers had been killed in the War, but there was one who had been living in Canada. He had died a year ago and left all his money to his two children. They would be about my own age, and like a good many of our present generation were completely indifferent to the rela-tionship, and all correspondence was dropped after the death of my uncle, so we had no one really we could turn to. We couldn't sell the boat either, before we'd finished it, and in any case we didn't want to as our heart and soul had gone into the job. I had even carved a figurehead, a wooden seal with mother of pearl eyes, and hanging flippers. His whiskers were made from fine copper wire, and we called him Ròn, the Gaelic name for 'seal'.

The rain was still beating on the glass roof, and the place felt eerie and chill. I gulped back a self-pitying tear, and then turned round abruptly to reach for another tool. As I did so my heart stopped and my blood ran cold . . . for I was standing face to face to a tall thin elderly man, with vivid blue eyes. He seemed unreal . . . wax-like; his face was yellow, and his hair showing under his broad brimmed hat was longish, tufted and coarse, like frayed manilla rope. His clothes were very old-fashioned too, and he spoke with what I thought at first was a Highland accent.

'Can I help you?' I said, when I had recovered from the shock of seeing him so close to me in this dimly lit deserted workshop.

'No, Ma 'am, no one can,' he said, 'I just couldn't rest till I saw for myself once more . . . so the old building's coming down at last . . . my, my, well, maybe it's for the best. I used to work on that bench hour in, hour out, till my back were nigh broke. You're doing a good job here yourself, Mary,' he said, lifting my mother's sewing table lid.

'How did you know my name was Mary?'

'Nothing to it, Mary . . . woman in a carpenter's shop . . . natural conclusion.'

'That's wicked.'

'Sure I'm wicked; I'm a wicked old man, and I just can't rest in peace, I always have to be poking around . . . I helped to build this place nigh on sixty years ago last fall.'

'Are you a Canadian then?'

'Yep, but I didn't go to Canada till I was seventeen . . . You've been crying, Mary, it disturbed me; tears are drops of life, they should not be shed wantonly. Reserve them, keep moist, don't wither up and shrink, parched and dry like me!'

'Who are you?' I demanded tensely . . . he must have some identity.

'I am Mercury, a messenger, a crosser of gulfs, a filler of chasms . . . a patron of actors and thieves. Do you see that little sparrow in the nest up there? She is sitting on three eggs. Two she will hatch, and they will try to use their wings too soon; they will stagger to the edge of the nest and fall to their doom . . . You will find their little bodies on this cement floor. The third one will hatch later, be stronger and will sail out into the light. But two must die first. Then you'll hear of me again.' The last sentence came out of him like from the Oracle, as if it had a double meaning.

I shuddered. My limbs felt limp and heavy. I moved slowly away from him to find a seat, to put some sacks on an old crate and take the weight off my feet. I felt faint; with an effort I turned my head towards him again saying, 'You haven't told me who you are . . . are . . . are – where are you – where have you gone?'

There was no sign of him, no noise, no shadow, nothing; he had completely disappeared, like a phantom. Was he a phantom? I was afraid to move. Petrified, I stayed quite still for what seemed like hours. Then mercifully Kazik came in through the door. I rushed towards him and threw my arms around him, 'I've just seen a ghost,' I said.

'Nonsense! How do you mean, a ghost?'

'Yes, yes it must have been. It must have been my uncle that died last year . . . you remember? In Canada, I'm convinced of it. He said he was "Mercury", well, Mercury was a sort of messenger, wasn't he? He also said that two little birds from the nest up there would fall out and die; but the third one, would survive and fly away, or rather "sail" away.'

'Cohannia, you've worked yourself flat out, you're exhausted, let us go home now and make supper; we have just got enough for a bottle of Bacchus. Come on, Cohannia, let us go home!'

Some weeks after that I forgot all about the old man and his prophecies, dismissed them from my mind. Kazik got a temporary job and I took a part-time job in a dress shop to try to accumulate enough money to launch our boat. So it came as a surprise and a bit of a shock one Saturday morning, when I went to the workshop and there, lying in the sawdust at my feet were the two little bodies of the newly hatched birds . . . through a hole in the wall a shaft of sunlight pointed straight at them. It was true then, what the old man had said.

I buried them gently under the roots of an old rotten tree outside the building, and quoted a verse from *Hamlet* over them, and wondered, what did it all mean? Next day, Sunday, another little bird was hatched. I watched it struggle to the edge of the nest getting stronger and more enterprising every minute. Kazik and I fixed an old fishing net above the floor level so that it would not fall to its doom like the other two . . . but there was no need; when it found the purpose of its wings it flapped them wildly and was borne off, following the sunlight to the outside world.

What would happen now? We waited expectantly; would Mercury turn up again? Or what?

Two weeks passed, and one Sunday afternoon a friend of ours telephoned . . . 'Hello, Mary,' she said, 'you will probably think I'm daft, but there's a notice in the personal column of the newspaper I'm just reading, perhaps you've seen it? It reads, "Would any descendant of the late Donald MacLeod who died in Canada last year kindly communicate,

85

as it would be to their advantage?" and it gives the address of the solicitor. . . . Well, he was your uncle, wasn't he?'

Needless to say I wrote immediately, and received a prompt reply from the solicitors informing me that my two cousins had been killed in a motor car accident, outright, and that I as next of kin stood to inherit quite a bit of money according to The Will of the Late Donald MacLeod; that is, if I were indeed Mary, the daughter of Mary MacLeod, sister of the late Donald MacLeod deceased.

So this was the riddle solved at last: the two little birds that were killed, my cousins; and the one that would 'sail away', me! And that is just what I did do; the boat was launched with part of the money and we sailed off at last 'over the sea to Skye'. Where we hope we shall live happily ever afterwards. And when the gulf is filled and the chasm crossed . . . who knows? I may have an opportunity of thanking Mercury himself . . . personally.

Relativity of Time

To fill time is to absorb time; the more we put into it the less we have of it. The more we agitate the sooner we are burnt out. In the middle years tomorrow, yesterday and today are all one, merged; we are cycling so fast that we can't see the wheels go round, then we seem to back pedal. The days are longer and the nights are endless.

So it was with Farquhar Anderson, known in the Gaelic as Fearchar Ruadh. He had always been an enterprising, energetic wee man;* before he left home he had built a fine house for his mother and left everything ship-shape, and he could now go to seek his fortune with an easy conscience. So off he went to Canada, and after two years working fruitlessly, and grimly hard up in the Yukon in the years of the Depression, he moved on to Australia and tried his hand at the sheep farming, equally without success. He lacked education, you see, and was no match for the wily merchants and big established farmers. So, he worked his passage home again, to find his mother was dead and his home that he had built was swarming with his brother's kids. You see, when his brother got married he didn't expect to set eyes on Fearchar again, so he took over his inheritance, the croft, the home, everything. Poor Fearchar was no match for him, either. He

* wee man – an odd-job man (Sc)

could reclaim nothing and in a fit of depression moved off to find another place for himself. He took the boat (it was his, anyway) and sailed off to find another island.

After three days sailing in rough and troubled waters, he struck the Orkneys; a shiny translucent sea splattered all over with green and fertile islands. He took his pick. The one he chose had once been peopled by a large community, it seemed. There were broken-down houses here and there, some with three walls and a chimney still protruding out of the nettles and dockens that frequently cosset an old, abandoned home. He made his way to one of these down beside a river. The river was in full spate and there were large flat stepping stones across it and at the other side he saw an ancient woman carrying a creel of peats, her burden was heavy and she seemed hesitant to cross. Fearchar leapt over the stones to her aid.

'Let me take that,' he said, relieving her of the creel.

'Thank you, my son, you are very kind, and a stranger to these parts, no doubt. Just you carry my creel to my hut and you will be rewarded . . . rewarded, re- . . . sin agad e*, sin agad e,' and she muttered on to herself like a cracked disc on an old gramophone, part in English and part in Gaelic, as she led the way to a black tarred wooden hut half hidden by a hillock, the path all scraped away by the energy of hens that perched now sleepily on the branches of a skeleton tree.

Inside the place was dark and paved with stone slabs, and a leather canopy vainly tried to direct the smoke of a glowing peat fire. It astonished Fearchar to find that her main furnishings were books, hundreds of them all round the walls and

* sin agad e – that's it

on the floor. 'There's nothing like the learning,' she said, 'it's food, meat and wine for me . . . Aye, aye, seagh gu dearbh.'*

Nevertheless, she brewed a mug of tea so strong, like treacle, and offered him a ship's biscuit to eat with it. Fearchar was too kind to refuse, and as the liquid was warm at least it released his tongue. He was soon chatting the old girl up telling of all his adventures abroad.

'And what will you be doing now?' said the cailleach.

'I want to rebuild one of these houses here, develop the land, start all over again.'

'Oh aye, huh, how old are you, my son? You have not much time, eh, I'm thinking.'

'I know,' said Fearchar dejectedly, 'time is the enemy.'

'Depends on how you look at it,' said the cailleach, 'time might be the friend . . . the friend, aye, aye.'

'How do you mean?'

'Take this stone with a hole in it, and this bit of string, and this bottle and this wee bag of seeds, and . . .'

'What, what for?' said Fearchar, looking at the sort of objects he carried in his pockets as a little boy . . . string, a bottle of water and a stone with a hole in it. 'What am I to do with these?'

'Listen then: tie the string to the stone, and when you have selected the ground you want to cultivate and build on, pause there and drink the liquid from the bottle, then wave the stone on the string three times round your head and don't move till you have counted up to ninety-nine . . . more doesn't matter, but you cannot count less, do you understand? . . . no less, no less, no . . .'

* seagh gu dearbh – to be sure, that's right

89

'Yes, yes,' said Fearchar intrigued and eager to try out any experiment that would break his run of rotten luck. So that same day, towards evening, found him standing in the middle of a fertile bit of land that swept right down to the sea. He could see his boat swinging at anchor, and the sea birds diving and swooping between the rocks. Everything was murmuring, swaying and swishing like the long grass tickling his bare feet. He stood motionless, a fine drizzle sprinkling his face.

This then was his utopia, his paradise; this was where he would build his new home. He drank the liquid entirely, proposing himself a toast; it tasted more like wine than water but maybe that was wishful thinking. Then he swung the stone three times round his head and proceeded to count: one, two, three, four – the wind had slackened – five, six, seven, eight – the murmuring ceased, the clouds widely grinning had captured the rain, the whole world fell silent, everything stood still. The birds were comically suspended, arrested in their flight, like surprised question-marks hung sideways. Even the fish must have halted, unable to move in the vast frozen masses of the sea. He saw his boat giddily balanced on the edge of a wave, its sails deflated, its flag square and solid like a postage stamp. The only living thing that could move was himself. He began to walk as though on air, half suspended, a puppet on a string. He reached a well but there was no water coming from its iron pipe; he found an old cottage with its fireplace and smoorings still there, the fire unkindled since many a long day. He looked again for the old woman's hut, and sure enough she was still there. 'There is no water coming from the pipe at the well. How do I live without water?'

'Ach, aren't I the stupid one,' she squawked. 'Wave the stone, lad, it will give you everything you want, including time . . . time . . . ach, aye! That's what everyone wants, time . . . time, but everything is dead here now, everything waits for you, lad. Everything, and when you are finished and have all you want, then reverse the numbers and throw away the stone! And by the way, don't look for me again as I won't be here. Bi falbh a niste.* Good-bye and good luck!' And she drifted away back into her smoke-filled room.

Feverishly, Fearchar waved the stone all over the land he had claimed, and true enough fine crops grew up. He rebuilt a discarded plough and likewise a house, a wheelbarrow, furniture and everything he wanted. He had worked hard and at last he was satisfied, so he went to the top of the hill and swung the stone again, this time reversing the numbers as the cailleach had said . . . and suddenly all came alive again! Once more gigantic waves leapt up on the shores, his crops of golden corn rhythmically swished in a strong sea breeze. The confused clouds streaked past no longer amused, the sea birds resumed their flight and swooped to find the fish, all unheeding and perplexed, a sure and vulnerable prey.

Wiping the drizzle from his brow, he ran down hell for leather to his boat and lifted anchor. He must visit another island to tell everyone of his good fortune. That same evening he sailed into Kirkwall harbour, where he met some fishermen and went to a ceilidh.

'Oh, so you are the fine fellow that was seen going ashore on the Isle of Spooks, eh? Man, I wish I had your courage, I wouldn't set foot on that place for all the tea in China.'

* bi falbh a niste – on you go now

'Why ever not?' said Fearchar.

'Well, they say you lose all sense of time there, man, and who can afford to do that? And that's not all they say, by a long shot. Ach, come on, man, you're not looking yourself at all, at all; what about another wee dram? . . . Give us your glass!'

And it was early morning by the time Fearchar sailed back to his island in a very different frame of mind, to find, as the Kirkwall fishermen had implied, nothing there . . . nothing, not even the little black witch on the stepping stones.*

* When Kazik and I sailed to Orkney and Shetland I was told by the local fishermen that there was an island where nobody would set foot . . . it was a magic place with lots of wee dangerous islands, and on one of these . . . if somebody had in the family a mentally defective child or a grown-up that they wanted hidden away, because they did hide them away, they would take them over to this island and tie them to a rock and let them finish their lives in that way. So the fishermen said, believe it or not; that was the story they told Kazik and I over a dram in all the frequent pubs we went to in Orkney, wonderful pubs.

Windfall

If you know the Shetland Isles at all you will know that there is not much in the way of trees growing on them. This is understandable since the completely unhindered Atlantic gales (straight from Canada) that break on these shores leave nothing unharmed, they tear up the rocks in great mouthfuls and regurgitate them back accompanied by such froth and spume that even the seals scuttle inland for protection. No wonder then that there have been many wrecks, many hulks of ships thrown up . . . but not abandoned, for the wood, if it is any use at all is immediately collected and used for making drunken-looking gates, all listing to the one side still retaining the shape of ships' timbers. The wooden barrels too, with a bite out of the one side and lid lowered make enchanting little seats.

But there are limits to this wood scavenging, for when Johnnie the Post wanted to use a big schooner called the *Mon Amour* that had been washed right up to the end of his croft, the local fishermen became quite agitated. 'You'll need to get permission from the salvage people,' they said, 'and it's not worth the trouble; you could poke your fingers right through her hull, can you not see she's rotten, man? Why, she has been lying there for more than half a century!'

Johnnie, you see, was still a stranger in the community; no one knew much about him since he came over from Caithness about eight or nine years ago, he was a deep one at that and a terror for reading books. The old wreck he was so determined to own had belonged at one time to a French explorer, and they were getting quite a laugh up at the post office, listening to Johnnie frantically trying to get in touch with the coastguard about his *Mon Amour*.

'You'll need to communicate with the General Receiver of Wrecks in Glasgow,' advised the coastguard, thinking him daft of course. But Johnnie didn't mind what they thought, he was getting the calls for nothing anyway, him being a postie, you understand.

Well, through time he got a reply giving him permission to own the boat for a fee of one pound sterling . . . 'provided that he would fully dispose of it'.

Imagine, where was the sense in that? The man was surely crazy to go on with it . . . it was not as though he were a handy man either, his wee house was falling round his ears. Every evening the local fishermen filled their pipes and sat on the dyke to speculate and ridicule his efforts, and the kids capered and yelled and danced around while Johnnie made a fine big bleezag on the shore, tearing the rotten ribs, decking, wheelhouse and floorboards apart to feed the flames.

It was not until the fire had eaten well down to the ballast that the men on the dyke really began to sit up and take notice . . . for this was no ordinary ballast . . . in fact right now there was a smart-looking Land Rover making its way down the rocky shore road and two strange men got out. They very carefully proceeded to select about a ton of the ballast which they carried off without a word.

Not long after that there was a noticeable change in Johnnie. He assumed the bearing and characteristics of a man of property, and indeed that is exactly what he became, building a fine guest house, licensed an' all, which he called the Cutty Sark.

But not so the locals: to them it is known as the Silver Ballast, and Johnnie himself as the Laird. 'No flies on that one,' you'll hear them mutter as they stagger home along the shore road – scanning their eyes for salvage.

Cold Comfort

It's not too wise to go by the weather forecasts in this country, I find. Far better to conclude that it's going to rain anyway, and count yourself lucky if it doesn't. I sometimes wonder if there is a wee invisible joker sitting on the weatherman's shoulder, determined to take the mickey out of us.* Mind you, it can't be easy to make a very accurate prediction 'cause if it's raining in London, then there is almost sure to be a heatwave in the North. For instance, a couple of winters ago they were sunbathing in the Isle of Lewis while the folk in Cornwall were digging their cars out of deep snow, and I have heard tales of bicycle tyres sticking to the wooden pier at Scalloway harbour in Shetland: it must have been a rare summer that all the same. For by and large it's the Sassenachs who get all the good sun, while we up North, especially in the Western Hebrides, cocoon ourselves in thick home-woven tweed, excellent whisky and traditional indifference to climate. Who wants hot weather anyway?

Mind you, there was a dear old codger in Skye once who made himself a pot of marmalade from a couple of oranges he had managed to grow in Armadale. 'Marmalade from Armadale!' he'd say. He was a bit of a poet too, you see, and what he didn't know about the mysterious movements of the

---

* take the mickey . . . – insult us, make a mockery of the Islands

Gulf Stream was nobody's business. 'After all,' he would argue, 'we can grow a palm or two in Uist. And the hydrangea are magnificent out there; it's all due to the warm effect of the Gulf Stream you see, and talking of heat reminds me of a fellow called Seabhas. He was a great storyteller, do you remember him by any chance?'

'Doctor Seabhas, the Sinn Feiner? Yes, I remember tell of him, a bit before my time though, surely?'

'Naturally, naturally,' said the old man trying to cover his indiscretion (for he was what is known as one of 'nature's gentlemen') . . . 'and this here story he told is a bit before anyone's time. It took place even before Robert the Bruce discovered the spider . . . You know of course that Seabhas was an Irishman as his name implies . . . his stories therefore might not be entirely based on fact.'

'You can talk,' I muttered, but fortunately he didn't hear me and I let him ramble on. The story then was about a certain King O'Donnell who had seven beautiful daughters. (Well, that's not quite accurate: it was six beautiful daughters and one plain one.)

'Well, as you probably know it was the parents who arranged the marriages of their daughters in those far-off days . . . And this King O'Donnell was a very busy man, as kings usually are, and a great disciplinarian: he would have his seven daughters all lined up every night to see that there were none of them missing. His method was to have seven gilded oil lamps put on the big oak table, and he would wait till each girl came in, sang a wee song and collected her own lamp, then went off to her bed . . . Later on he would take the precaution to have the stables checked to see that there were none of the seven horses missing. He had given them

97

one each, for he was a genial, good-hearted sort of fellow, really, you know.

'But in spite of all his efforts one of them, his youngest, escaped and sailed away to England (or was it Scotland)? Anyway, believe it or not, she married with one of your own ancestors. Ha! You see, you didn't know you had royal Irish blood in you, did you now?'

'Well, there's Irish blood, and *Irish* blood,' said I, 'but I've got a splash of it right enough.'

'Quiet then,' the old man continued . . . 'The King, for reasons of his own (him being a great horse fancier) would consult with his friend, the aforesaid ancestor of Seabhas, about eligible suitors for his daughters, preferably those owning a good stud; and he was reasonably successful, ladies of royal blood being few and far between in Ireland even in those days, and they were lovely looking creatures . . . except for the elder one, Bridget, and even Seabhas had to agree, there was no one in all Ireland that would give good horses for her.

"Sure I'll tell you what," said the King, "what about setting sail for some of those small islands in the Western Hebrides? You're sure to find someone for her there; judging by the yarns our warriors bring back, the men up there must be in a terrible state of frustration. Just look at the names they've given their mountains: the Paps of Caithness, the Maidens of Morvern, Beinn na Caillich, the Seven Sisters – there's one for you now – and our Bridget's surely better-looking than one of those lumpy-looking mountains!"

'So forthwith, his friend Seabhas was commissioned to set off on his travels by land and by sea, and the slightly embellished description he gave of poor Bridget roused no emotion whatsoever in any Highlander's heart. Ultimately he reached the most northerly parts, the perry-ferry of the land . . .'

'Periphery, do you mean?' I broke in.

'Periphery – perry-ferry – take your pick, but don't interrupt! . . . Where was I now?'

'Well, you did start talking about heat and the weather, but you – some –'

'Oh, aye, that's it: about heat' . . . (and he was back once more in his stride). 'Well, at last he arrived in a place in the freezing North where they had no kind of fuel whatsoever (or women) to keep them warm. The forests had all been burnt down by the clansmen indulging in their usual feuds. And this lot had been defeated so badly, there was just a handful of them left, wounded, unhappy and dying of cold.

'Their leader, a handsome young prince, leaned over his dying father's bier . . . (or maybe I should say byre?) and gently closed his eyes. Then taking up his father's sword he strode away, leaving his men all huddled round the only remaining cauldron of steaming boiling water, into which they dipped their long tartan plaids, then squeezing them out wrapped themselves tightly before going to sleep.'

'Well, that's one way of keeping warm,' I ventured timidly.

'Uist, you besom, be quiet, I'm not done yet!' he scolded.

'And the young prince walked down by the white sands, the shadow of his slim limbs and his fine sword following behind him. Then he stopped and raised his arms to the Moon God.

"An ainm an Dhé," he moaned aloud, "cuidich mi!"* Then he went and found for himself a cave and went to sleep in it.

* an ainm an Dhé . . . cuidich mi – in the name of God, help me

99

And in the middle of the night he was wakened by an apparition, a sort of fish man, with gleaming fins and a golden crown . . . a crossing between his own father and Neptune, King of the Sea.

> "Get up my son," It commanded
> "And use your ancient sword
> That was once mine and is now yours
> Go you to where the men are sleeping
> And close by you will see a rock
> With a black cleft in it
> Waken your men and tell them to follow you
> Bringing a burning faggot
> Command them to dig in the cleft
> And tunnel down deep
> For there inside it you will find
> All the riches and treasure of the world
> And they will be yours
> And you will have a great and lifelong following
> Go now!"

'And he drifted through the mouth of the cave, back towards the sea. And the young prince, without hesitation, made his way in the darkness to where the men were sleeping, so strongly did he believe what he had been told.

"Arise," he shouted, "éirich a sin thu! Follow me, and bring what tools you can find!" Then by the light of a feeble faggot, he saw before him, not many strides away, the aforesaid rock.

'And as the men all gathered round him, bedraggled and shivering in their damp plaids, he ordered them to start digging . . . but nothing happened. "Dig again . . . deeper," he yelled, and they dug and dug obediently, not knowing why.

"He's surely daft or drunk," they whispered together. "It will be the death of his father . . . or maybe the Moon, poor fellow." And being of noble fiery blood the young prince didn't like it at all, at all. So, clutching his sword tightly, he started slashing at random, exhausting himself. The men meanwhile kept clear of him and taking advantage of the breather, started trying to rekindle the fire, using the lumps of rock they had dug up to support the cauldron.

'The young prince was so incensed by their remarks, and his own failure to find the fortune, that he seized a burning torch and flinging it towards the men yelled, "Take that, a Mhic an Sad, you blundering glaoichs that dig like women!"

'And suddenly clouds of blue smoke began to stream out of the lumps around the cauldron, causing an acrid sort of smell. Then beautiful flames reached out from the smoke, and a great heat began to develop . . . "Taing dhan a dh'earrach, taing dhan a dh'earrach," the warriors yelled, (meaning 'thanks to the Moon God').

'And as they danced around the cauldron they tore their plaids to ribbons in their wild excitement. For you do realise what they had discovered? . . . It was –'

'I know, don't say it . . . it was coal.'

'Ach damn'ity, how did you guess?'

'Well, coal was probably discovered around the eleventh century in Scotland, wasn't it?'

'Ach, I suppose so. But nevertheless, you're a bit too clever for my liking.'

'Never mind . . . wait a bit though, you never told me who Seabhas got for poor Bridget . . . The prince I suppose?'

'Ach, that's not very likely . . . for the Highlanders are very choosey, you see.'

'Indeed, and don't I just know it!' said I.*

* It's taken from a story my father told me as fact: in Ireland it was Archdeacon King who had seven daughters, he had a candle for each of them laid out on the spinet piano which my father inherited, and this night when the girls came down King noticed the end candle had not been taken, so the household and servants and everyone were alerted to find out what'd happened to Sarah, the youngest, and they discovered that she was missing altogether and so was one of the grooms. And the story my father told was that they'd managed to run away to Liverpool, Sarah and this groom called O'Donnell and they married, and my father maintained that we're descended, that I'm descended from them. Whether Sarah, the youngest daughter of the Archdeacon King, eloped with O'Donnell or not, that's what my father told me as fact.

The Pied Piper

It is many a long day since Donald put the weirdie pipes*
upon the shelf above the mantelpiece and swore never to use
them again, not outside anyway. It was all right if you blew
on them inside the house – you could come to no harm there
– but somehow he knew that to blow them outside was
asking for trouble. It was dangerous, they could lead you into
all sorts of misadventure; for these pipes had seen many a
hard battle lost and won, but the men who blew on them had
never lived to bring them back home again.

Donald was a lonely man and getting on in years. He was
also a little bent with rheumatics, which he had learnt to live
with. He treated his rheumatism as a sort of built in barom-
eter; he could tell when it was going to rain or when he was in
for a dry spell. His three apple trees growing from the
cracked flagstones in front of his thatched cottage would
tell him anything else he needed to know, about the seasons,
or the changing light for fishing, and many things besides. He
would talk to them often like they were old friends; in fact at
this very moment he was prattling away about the vapours
rising from the frogspawn in the ditch down by his gate.

'Do you think that's bad for my chest, maybe?' he would
ask them.

* the weirdie pipes – uncanny Scottish bagpipes

'Ach, no-ooo,' murmured the trees, in the way trees do.

'Should I dig a trench to drain it down to the road, maybe?'

'Rather you than me,' said a strange, real voice in his ear, and he nearly jumped out of his skin with fright. Turning round he saw a tall, thin man in tweed knickerbockers, carrying a camera (a tourist no doubt).

'Oh, you gave me quite a start,' said Donald, 'I didn't see you coming. Is there anything I can do for you?'

'Well, I wondered if I might take a snap of your cottage?'

'Certainly!' said Donald; 'do you want myself standing in front of it?' He was getting used to these tourists and their cranky capers, but he was always willing to oblige. He was proud of his little cottage with its fire on the hearth, American rocking-chair and brass spittoon. When he had finished posing for the camera, hand on hip, he would invite the stranger in. 'Bend your head,' he warned, as he led the way from the sunlight outside into a densely peat-smogged room.

Well, it was not long before Donald and the Englishman (for that's what he turned out to be) were on the best of terms, drinking strong tea and eating ship's biscuits,* and prattling away about Donald's days in the merchant navy and the Sassenach's days of digging and desperation as an air raid warden in the London Blitz. He said he had lost his wife and four children in one of those raids, and he had come North to try to learn to live again, 'recuperate' his doctor had called it . . . Donald looked into his eyes and they both knew that that was impossible.

'Shall I play you a tune on the pipes to cheer you up?' said

* ship's biscuits – big quarter-inch thick biscuits containing caraway seed, tasty and brittle, introduced to Skye by the sailors and sold in my grandmother's wee shop

Donald impulsively. (He could have bitten his tongue off for the rashness of his words.)

'Please do,' said the Sassenach.

And so Donald blew the dust off the box and began to assemble the pipes, a feeling of misgiving and foreboding heavy in his heart. Once or twice he tried to back out. 'The bag is a bit dry,' he said, 'it needs treating.'

'Oh, how do you do that, Donald?' asked the man.

'Well, usually rubbing it with a mixture of honey and whisky does the trick, but the honey I gave to a sick cow and the whisky I'm afraid got finished at the New Year. Perhaps I could play them another time?'

'Oh, no, please don't disappoint me now!' pleaded the Sassenach.

'Ach, well then, mind you it's an awful noise in this wee room.'

'Well then, couldn't we go outside?'

'Oh, dear me, no,' said Donald, 'man, not with these pipes,' and there was a distant look in his eyes that puzzled his visitor.

So it was then that Donald did play a tune for the poor man, in spite of himself, and the Sassenach was so taken with it that he decided to learn to play the pipes himself. He came up every day to learn from Donald, and proved to be a very apt pupil. It was not very long before he could play as well as Donald himself.

Round and round the little kitchen they marched, pitter-em-pattering away for all they were worth . . . Mind you, it was not all Highland tunes they played; Donald was always fair, and he let the Sassenach go his dinger* with tunes like

* go his dinger – practise very vigorously (Sc)

105

'Home Sweet Home' and 'Riding down from Bangor', not that he had any liking for them himself (God knows)!

There was only one thing that troubled Donald. The big stranger kept on trying to get through the door with the pipes and play them outside, and that Donald knew would be disastrous. It was no use trying to explain to a Sassenach that the pipes were fey, and had a will of their own and that they would lead him into danger, as they had led his own father, his grandfather and for the matter of that, his great-great-grandfather. The man would just laugh at him.

And then, one day, the music went to the Sassenach's head altogether; he was fairly carried away with himself. He shoved Donald aside, and barged through the door, playing 'Hey Johnnie Cope are ye waken yet?' fit to burst. Down the road he went, striding it out, with old Donald hardly able to catch up with him.

Now it so happened that the local school was just letting out its pupils for the day; out they came, tumbling and shoving like a river in full spate, and when they saw the piper there was no stopping them. They tagged on behind him like a regiment of soldiers, and started marching away up the main road towards Kyleakin.

Now in those days part of the old wooden pier was still standing at Kyleakin and it was pretty rotten; but the Sassenach was not to know that, and before you could say 'knife' or anyone could stop him, he was away to the end of it, all the children running behind him. Well, whether it was the weight of the lot of them or just the age of the rotten wood, or just the curse that had been put on the pipes, no one will ever know. Whatever it was, it was a sad fate the poor man suffered when a plank fell from under his feet, and he went down, heavy boots, knickerbockers, and the water gurgling from the drones of the pipes . . . to be swept and carried far out by the swift tides running in the narrows of the Kyles. The children, by the grace of God, ran back in horror, and were saved.

Donald missed his Sassenach friend for many a long day, although he was heartily glad to be rid of the pipes. Mind you, there were times when he was sure he heard them playing 'Hey Johnnie Cope, are ye waken yet?' as he blethered away to his trees in front of his cottage door.

The Balbhan

The midwife looked perturbed when the second twin met the light of day. It didn't cry out like the first one, and although in every other respect it was identical and very much alive, there was surely something wrong, and within a week sure enough the local doctor confirmed: one of Kate Finlayson's twin boys was a deaf mute, but a fine-looking little fellow with gold hair and blue eyes and sound in every other way.

Not so long ago the Outer Hebrides were very inaccessible. Kate Finlayson was poor and the earnings of her fisherman husband erratic, so there was very little she could do for the unfortunate one, who became known locally as 'the Balbhan'. He did not go to school with his brother, but they taught him all they could at home, helped greatly by a cousin of Kate's, a retired medical missionary home from Uganda. He even managed to teach him languages let alone to read and write; and, being a great wee mimic, the Balbhan would copy his brother Finlay's every move and gesture. They were so close you would think they had only the one mind between them. They cared deeply for each other and were passionately loyal, the one rising to defend the other instinctively as twins often do. Heaven help any other boy who would throw a stone at or in any way annoy the Balbhan; Finlay would be at their throat with a vengeance. They had their own way of communicating with each other, by touch, drawings and acting; it was fantastic to watch them playing and working in such perfect unison. Next to each other their best friends were the animals, even the wild deer didn't run away from them; the Balbhan could walk in amongst them as they lay deep in the bracken in seemingly motionless masses, sleeping, anticipating, listening, who can tell? The birds, too, would flutter down beside him if he rested at the edge of a field after a hard day's work, for he could work very intelligently even though he couldn't form a single word; he was especially good in the hills at rounding up the sheep.

Now there was one pastime the twins couldn't really share fully together, and that was Finlay's inordinate love of the sea. The Balbhan couldn't hear it for one thing, and Finlay found it hard to describe. His longing to (one day) sail away out there without his brother hurt him sorely – they would paddle down the knobbly burns that led to the sea, and sit for hours popping the seaweed which the Balbhan enjoyed even though he couldn't hear a single pop; for Finlay would describe to him in writing or by gesture all about the throbs and murmurs of the scuttling crabs and crick-crack of the razor fish, but he had no way of imparting his love for the sea; it was too large, too massive. And when he was fifteen, torn and anguished though he was to leave his brother, he nevertheless packed up and joined the merchant navy.

The poor Balbhan was beside himself with grief; no one could console him; the local undertaker (meaning it kindly enough) even got him to collect dry hay to make mattresses for the coffins 'to take him out of himself', but the poor Balbhan could put no heart into the work and took himself off to the shieling where he and Finlay had had their own hut. He would spend all summer there, coming back only when his brother was home on leave.

Then he would come alive again, jubilant, ecstatic, jumping and dancing and twirling round like a monkey on a hurdy-gurdy. He loved dressing up in Finlay's uniform, and indeed he looked fine in it. They both did (separately of course), and they got a great kick out of playing tricks on other people, the one posing as the other.

One autumn when their father was laid up with bronchitis and Finlay was home on leave there was a great spate of herring, a glut of them in fact; they were throwing them back in the sea in Stornoway, and the old man was writhing in his bed at not being able either to crew for anyone or to take his own boat; it was a big loss of money.

'Leave it to me,' said Finlay, 'I've got a long leave and I'll have the nets out tomorrow night!' and he was as good as his word. He was also in luck. The hold was full to the gunwales, but when he got in to Stornoway the prices the buyers were offering were lower than ever, so he found himself involved in heated arguments, stimulated by excessive drinking in the bars; and after about a week of it, his head somewhat blurred, he was approached by a gentleman, a real gentleman, not one of those Union sharks, 'Let me fill your glass,' he said. 'No use looking at a shallow bottom.'

After a while Finlay focused sufficiently well to notice that the man wasn't drinking himself. 'That won't do, where's your glass, man? Fill him up there, Angus!'

'Oh, no, no thank you, you see I daren't!'

'What do you mean, you daren't?' said Finlay, trying to fix him.

'It's my wife, she's raising hell and all merry about having to wash her smalls in salt water. I went to the chemist for some detergent for her, and now I find I am unavoidably detained ashore.'

'Oh, you're off that cruiser out in the bay! Ach, man why didn't you say so . . . Have another wee snifter!'

'No, you see what I wanted to ask you . . . would it be an awful imposition to get you to take it out to her? I think that's your boat moored close to ours . . . the *Rhona Mary*, is that it?'

'That's it, the very one, called after my mother . . . Certainly, you're on, boy, oh . . . any time you like . . .'

'Well, now would be as good as any . . . they're closing anyway.'

So Finlay took the packet from the man and shoved it in his uniform pocket – making it quite difficult to fasten the buttons over his seaman's jersey. And they staggered down the slippery jetty to where his dinghy was tied.

'Don't forget now!' shouted the man. 'Just give the detergent to Madame Leighton, she'll be waiting for it (and tell her to use the red rinse – red rinse, got that)?' And giving the dinghy a shove off with his foot he threw him the line, and was soon a small speck on the landscape.

Finlay rowed a zigzag course till he reached the launch, and boarding her started to yell, 'Anybody aboard? Permission to come aboard?' till a tall blonde (a real bobby dazzler) emerged from the aft cabin. 'Madame Satan, er, Lay, Leighton, I presume?' spluttered Finlay, bringing himself to a staggered attention and attempting a clumsy salute. When suddenly in the darkness her eyes seemed to expand . . . she turned abruptly and ran below again leaving Finlay rather stupidly holding the parcel.

Then, seemingly out of the darkness of the sea, two men suddenly pounced on him. 'We are Customs officers,' one of them said. 'All right, I'll take that . . . Come on, move!' and they shovelled him down into a waiting dinghy with an outboard. But fortunately for Finlay, as they got under way the sea turned nasty. And Finlay knew fine the frailty of this kind of boat, so, in a trice he jumped up and shoogled her till she capsized, and all three of them were in 'the drink'.

Finlay was a powerful swimmer, and was soon scrambling ashore. He was not only 'stone cold sober' by now, he was blooming well perished; but he daren't make for friends in the town . . . or for home, as he knew he hadn't got a leg to stand on, as far as clearing himself went. A merchant-navy man carrying narcotics aboard a strange yacht! What a fool he was letting himself be codded into thinking it was detergent! Suddenly he began to think about the Balbhan. It had happened before, this strong pull when he was in any kind of trouble . . . and from that he thought about the hut in the shieling. No one would find him there, and he would have time to think out what to do . . . So, audaciously he ran towards a shed behind the Customs house. There he knew he would find the exciseman's bicycle. Then three or four miles out of Stornoway he abandoned the bike, and made the rest of the way through the night on foot. By the time he reached the hut in the shieling it was already morning. He was dead beat and his clothes had dried on him.

It didn't surprise him at all to see the Balbhan sitting there waiting for him. His face showed all the concern that had driven him out of his bed, and drawn him instinctively towards the shieling where he knew full well he would find his brother. Slowly with his finger he traced a large question mark on the floor, then started to make some brose for them to eat.

On the edge of an old newspaper Finlay wrote briefly what had happened. He never held anything back from the Balbhan. Then throwing off his clothes he rolled himself in a blanket and went to sleep. Meanwhile, the Balbhan searched around the hut till he found an old writing pad on which he wrote,

Dear Fin,

Clear the country as fast as you can, and don't forget to write to me. I have envied you this uniform for long enough, now is my chance to feel what it's like to be a real man, experiencing real adventure. Don't try to stop me, you know as I do it's the only chance for both of us. After all they can't keep me long can they?

Cheerio,

Bally.

Then, placing his brother's cap at a jaunty angle on his head he buttoned up the jacket, and placed yet another note in the pocket to be handed to the two men he knew he would inevitably meet somewhere on the road to Stornoway. It read,

I will not utter a single word until I have seen a solicitor.

Needless to say he was dragged off to Inverness on the next boat that left the island, nor did he break his silence when he landed before the magistrate, or the psychiatrist. It was not till they got a specialist to him, thinking he was suffering from some kind of shock, that they realised he was a deaf mute. 'An interesting case,' commented the specialist, 'very interesting. This fellow could still be able to talk . . . it only needs a slight operation to restore his hearing . . . Pity we didn't get at him sooner.'

'And pity,' said the magistrate, 'that they didn't get at the other fellow sooner; he'll be out of the country by now.' And so he was, on his way to South America in fact.

Meanwhile the Balbhan rested peacefully in hospital, attended by such a pretty nurse, whom he afterwards married. She was an English girl, and they went to live in London somewhere near Heathrow Airport, for the Balbhan you see could now fully hear the noise of the aeroplanes, and how he loved it.

Finlay, too, had fallen in clover in South America (so to speak, for maybe it doesn't grow there). He'd married a Spanish girl whose father owned vineyards. He kept in constant touch with the Balbhan and sent him large sums of money; not that the Balbhan needed it, for he had started his own fish and chip shop. The fish was supplied direct from his father in Stornoway, not rock salmon you understand, but real salmon. Yes, Bally Finlayson's shop was renowned for its 'grilled salmon cutlets, and chips' . . . and wine of course!

The Hazel-nut Bridge

The smell of peat smoke was heavy in the small room, for in spite of all young Neilag's efforts he couldn't seem to rekindle the dying embers of the fire.* His sister Mairianna was crying again as she squatted beside him on the lumpy mud floor; every now and then she would pause and sniff and let her eyes trace and follow the pipe clay pattern that her granny had made round the edges of the floor. Her mother did that sometimes too. It was a sort of white lace design, a border of sweeping scallops topped with daisies.† She longed to have a bash at it herself, and now even more than ever she longed to go home.

'I want my mother,' she bawled out loud, and poor wee Neil tried to console her by distracting her attention.

'Look, look at Castle Moil,' he said, giving a big smouldering peat another vigorous poke. 'It's crumbling, falling down and smashing to pieces.'

'It's not Castle Moil, and it's not a bit like it either,' fretted Mairianna, 'and you'd better stop trying to poke that fire,

* This is a true story dedicated to the memory of my mother, Mairianna Macleod, and my Uncle Neil.
† Yes, well they did that a lot: after they had cleaned the house completely spick and span, they went down on their knees for ages with their pipe clay (which comes out white when you wet it) and they made wonderful patterns, squiggles, Grecian types and swastikas all round the edge of the black mud floor.

can't you see it's out? . . . And anyway what's the use . . . I think my granny must be dead . . . I'm sure she is,' and once again Mairianna gave out a fearsome wail, like a cow in labour.

'Why are you saying that she is dead?' whispered Neil in the next lull.

'Well, she's stopped snoring, hasn't she? . . . And she is not even breathing now.'

Neil raised himself from the floor laboriously and, taking his sister's hand in his he gave it a wee comforting squeeze. 'Uist, Mairianna, don't be frightened, amn't I still with you . . . but perhaps we'd better take a look at her all the same.'

Stealthily, on tiptoe, the two small children approached their grandmother's bed, in spite of the immense shadow of her profile stark against the whitewashed wall putting the fear of death on them; for although they loved their granny well enough, they were a little afraid of her and very homesick since they had been sent to stay in her little smoke-filled thatched cottage some nineteen miles from their own home, while their mother was expecting yet another child. It was the custom in those bygone days so to do.

The old woman lay motionless in her rough, pinewood bed, its neat canopy of red and white spotted gingham casting weird shadows across her ashen face, and there was not a cheep out of her. 'Feel her hand,' said Neil, 'to see if it's cold,' and Mairianna nearly jumped out of her skin at the loud sound of his voice.

'Shis, I can't . . . there's something heavy lying over it.'

'Ach, don't be daft, can't you see that that's just her own stomach lying down beside her?'

Voluntary Aid Despatchment nurse at the time of the
Clydebank Blitz, 1939.

Rhona as Alexandrina in 'The Gentle Art', in the doorway of her
great-grandmother's cottage, Breacais, Skye.

Rhona, husband Kazik (foreground) and friends sailing, 1964.

Lusa cottage on right, where Rhona lived from 1971–86.
In the background, Beinn na Caillich, near where Rhona now
lives in Broadford.

Rhona modelling her new gillie shoes.

Rhona, BBC Radio dramatist and storyteller.

'Teach Me To Waltz', an original painting by the author.
See 'The Gentle Art'.

'Mallaig Fishermen', an original painting by the author.

Grandmother Rebekah Mackinnon's original spinning wheel.
See 'Skye's the Limit'.

Mairianna drew back from the bed abruptly, starting to cry again and trying to drag her brother away towards the door with all the force that her small being could muster. 'We must go home . . . we must go home . . . come on – now . . . we can't stay here, we'll starve, and if anybody finds us they are sure to think we killed my granny on purpose . . . and, and . . .'

'Wait, wait a minute, we can't just run out into the night without even knowing where we are going,' said Neil.

'We can go to the woods at Skulamus, can't we, till my father comes to look for us . . . he's sure to come to look for us . . . and there's plenty hazel-nuts down by the Hazel-nut Bridge, my Uncle Donald told me so. And . . . and we can get plenty water to drink from the river . . .'

Reluctantly, Neil followed her out. Girls were always so bossy, especially Mairianna; it was easier to do as she said than to argue with her. Was his granny really dead, though? They would get a hell of a row for walking out in the middle of the night if she wasn't. Keeping to the soggy edge of the rough road they trotted briskly one ahead of the other, their bare feet numb, and swinging their arms like windmills from time to time in an effort to keep warm. Soon they came on the densely wooded slope by the river known as 'Skulamus' and ferreted their way in amongst the thickly tangled hazel bushes.

'This is great, isn't it?' said Mairianna, snuggling down in a recently vacated fox or sheep's lair, and looking for all the world like a little old banshee. 'Now you go off and get the nuts!' she ordered.

'Stad ort,' said Neil (which means, hold on), and he started scratching his head slowly, 'I'm after thinking . . . that maybe, this is the wrong time of the year for gathering nuts, anyhow.'

'A Mhic an Sad,'* Mairianna spat out at him in the Gaelic, 'my Uncle Donald said that you could always get nuts at Skulamus.'

'Well, he was a liar.'

'Oh Dia, would you listen to that, that's blasphemy, you'll go straight to hell for saying that . . . and you'll go to Hell anyway for killing my granny!' said Mairianna, jerking her head to the side quickly to avoid a possible slap, then starting to blubber just as though she had had it.

'I did not kill her . . . neither of us killed her . . . she just died by herself, and fine you know it!' shouted Neil angrily.

And as they argued bitterly the real night settled in darker than ever, for there was no moon to speak of, and the blackness soon enveloped them completely. Up till now, they had courage and purpose in what they did, but gradually the cold and hunger and fear brought them closer together, hardly daring to breathe for the noises of the night and the fear of the unknown . . . eerie shapes and noises coming from twisted arthritic knuckles of the brittle lichen-covered twigs crack-cracked, and the shiny silver spider web, now forming in their hair; the sound of the breeze gossiping and whispering in their ears, and the dew that shone on their lashes and mingled with their tears . . . 'Our Father Who art in Heaven, hallowed be Thy name,' began Neil as he tucked his sister's frozen hand up the sleeve of his jumper . . . 'Thy will be done, Thy kingdom come . . . or is it Thy kingdom come Thy will be done? . . . Ach, I forget, I'll just make it

* A Mhic an Sad – the Son of the Devil

like a letter – Dear God, please help us – yours sincerely, with love, amen, Neilag.' Then like his sister, he too fell fast asleep.

As the first light of dawn fought its way amongst the bushes the children woke and tried to move their frozen limbs; they crawled painfully down towards the river and sat for a while on the Hazel-nut Bridge. 'Isn't this a fairy bridge?' said Neil. 'Don't they say if you sit long enough, you'll see into the future?'

'I'm seeing into it now,' said Mairianna speaking like one still sleeping.

'You are not and . . . and if you are,' said Neil, 'what do you fancy you're seeing?'

'I'm seeing me, in a pink silk dress with tiny pearl beads on the bodice. It's a wedding – there's a big white cake – and I'm a bridesmaid . . . and . . . and I'm dancing in the first reel . . . and . . .'

'That's nothing,' broke in Neil, 'I'm seeing myself too,' and he narrowed his eyes mysteriously to gaze into space. 'It's a boat . . . my own boat, and I'm wearing wellington boots and a jumper. She's lying on a sea anchor . . . we've the boards out for the flat fish poaching . . . wait a minute though, we've been spotted. It's the snoopers, dhia beannaich sinn.* There's a five-hundred pound fine on that . . . cut the ropes and let the boards drift, man!' shouted Neil. 'Now heave the anchor! Heave – one two, heave – one two . . . ach, damn it, I slipped!'

'And you'll be in the river if you don't watch out!' interrupted Mairianna.

* dhia beannaich sinn – God bless us

'She's gaining on us fast,' breathed Neil . . . 'a big black craft with billowing sails bearing down on us.'

'Billowing sails my foot!' exclaimed Mairianna jumping down from the bridge excitedly, 'it's my granny – she's not dead after all. Look, look – listen, she's shouting for us, do you hear her?'

And sure enough in the far distance there was a figure emerging from out of the morning mist. It was a big woman in black, and getting even taller and bigger every minute and waving her long walking stick, for all the world like a swaying mast, and the skirts she wore billowing out as though they were fit to burst. 'As sure as death, you must have the Gift right enough,' said Mairianna (rather condescendingly) . . .

'And seemingly, so too have you,' said Neil a week later; for would you believe it, Seadan (the post) brought them a letter to say that they were to go back home at once – as Mairianna was needed – to be a bridesmaid at her sister Curstag's wedding.

A Sporting Chance

My grandfather Angus MacLeod died in 1906.* He had a long beard and a short temper and spent much of his time going to sea. In spite of all that he had a devoted wife and ten children; and when he died my grandmother continued to work the croft and mind their little shop and raise their large family and still maintain a good figure, pitch black hair and fine white skin – and although she was a brave and determined woman she could often be gentle, pensive and shy. My heart aches when I think how later in life she lost four of her fine sons in World War I, and she was left much alone with more than enough to do.

There was one wild night in the middle of the winter when she was late with the milking and hurrying out to the byre with the clanging pails and her milking stool, and the cat following close at her heels. As she approached the byre she was surprised to find the door wide open, the top half banging to and fro with the wind. She was sure she had closed it when she put the cows in. They seemed peaceful enough, though, all three of them – Té Ruadh (the red one), Té Thana (the thin one) and Leisgeadair (the lazy one) – she was lying down as usual. Rebecca (my grandmother) settled herself and started milking Té Ruadh, aiming the first squirt

* This story is true, every word of it.

121

of the milk at the cat as usual. (One has to give to get.) She felt a bit uneasy, and Té Thana sensed this in the way cows do. She had to tie its hind legs together, and the taking was poor. Perhaps she would have more luck with Leisgeadair . . . 'Éirich, éirich a Leisgeadair,' she urged as she tried to prod the old cow to its feet. Then she dropped her milk buckets and started to scream, for there, lying under the cow, was a man stark naked save for a bit of sacking round his loins!

Now, I said before that my grandmother was a very brave woman, so instead of running away she steeled herself and asked the stranger in Gaelic what he thought he was doing there, 'An ainm an Dhé, gu dé tha thu a'deanamh ann a sin?' There was no reply, so she tried English, and still no response . . . So she knelt down beside him to see if he was dead. Well, no, he wasn't. But what a state the poor man was in! He was as thin as a rake, with his eyes bloodshot and too weak to raise his head or his arms when she offered him some of the warm milk she poured into the lid of the pail. She ran to the house for some warm blankets and mixed a drop of Talisker whisky together with some meal, cream and honey. This he would take, she had no doubt . . . and he did; and then when he recovered sufficiently to move, he began to cower away from her like a frightened animal muttering all the while in a strange unknown language. So she went back to the house to find an old pair of trousers and a jersey and boots. These she left at the byre door together with a plate of scones and a bowl of hot soup.

Next morning the stranger was gone. There was neither sight nor sound of him . . . but in the soup bowl was a little silver ring with a miniature iron cross on it, and bearing the inscription GOTT-MIT-UNS.

A fortnight later the policeman was round. Rebecca thought at first he wanted to check the sheep dip. But when he had taken a cup of tea and warmed himself at the peat fire, he thrust his thumbs in his upper pockets and said, 'Did you hear there was a German prisoner of war missing from the Island of Raasay? He had been working the iron ore there. One of the others said they had seen him swimming out to sea . . . but of course you can't believe a word these bastards say.'

'Well, maybe aye and maybe uhn-uh,' said Rebecca, pouring out more tea. She never gave the German prisoner away, she was so sorry for him, but she had his ring for many years.

The Ring on the Tree

There was a bachelor living near to the town of Urray in Inverness-shire once. It was at the time of the Boer War, and like many another brave lad he had to drop all his future plans and his courting, and 'go to it'. But before he went he decided to clinch matters with Curstag his sweetheart and ask her to marry him, and he was sure she would say 'yes' to a handsome lad like himself. But, alas, I am afraid he was just a wee thing too confident. Anyway, one day when he went with some heifers to the Dingwall Market he found he got a surprisingly good price for them, much more than he ever expected, and so with the money he went and bought a beautiful gold ring for Curstag – a real bobby dazzler.*

Well, you can imagine his amazement and disappointment when she would have none of him! It was an awful slap in the eye for him, and made him very angry and unhappy, and he didn't know what on earth to do with the ring. One thing was sure though, he would give it to no other woman.

Soon the time came for his departure, and before getting into the gig with his white spats and long hairy sporran, he decided to go out to the old rowan tree that grew at the end of his croft, to ruminate and maybe take a ghost of the smell of it away with him. He twiddled the ring in his hands

* a real bobby dazzler – one brilliantly dazzling (Sl)

absently, then tried it on one of the small branches. It stuck, so he just left it there. What use had he for it now?

Well, to cut a short story even shorter . . . Many years passed, and when the war was good and truly over he returned to his empty croft to find his kith and kin all dead or departed, and nothing left that he had ever known save the old rowan tree; and lo and behold, there under its boughs stood Curstag, her still golden hair shining to match the hidden ring. The ring that had brought her back to him.

The Magic Willow

There was a young woman once and she was handsome according to the standards of her day. She lived near Elgin, Morayshire, and when she walked along the road the young men would gawk with admiration. Her bosom was so high you could balance a plate on it, and her hair was black and shiny as a hearse. But she was discontented. She had married with a fine man, but they had no children; then he died leaving her a poor, sad, lonely (but still beautiful) widow.

One very hot day, in the middle of July, she went to draw water from the slowly trickling well, and was surprised to find an old crippled woman with a stick standing close by. 'O, mo ghaoil 's math gun tàinig sibh,' she said in the Gaelic (Oh, my love, good that you came). Her trouble was that she was stiff with rheumatics and could not bend down to take a drink. The young woman, whose name was Giorsal, drew her some water without hesitation.

'Tapadh leibh, tapadh leibh,'* the old cailleach muttered her thanks, gulping noisily. Then she raised her stick and pointed to a willow tree, its silver leaves shimmering in the sun. 'For your kindness to a stranger,' said the cailleach, 'you can pick a leaf of yonder tree and turn it in your hand, then make a wish. But don't be greedy, for as sure as I'm standing

* tapadh leibh – thank you (with respect)

here, the wish will come true! Mind you, you'll have to work for it. Each leaf you pull is an idea, an inspiration, and it is for you to make or mar it.'

'Well, there was no harm in trying,' thought Giorsal, and she went to the tree the same evening. She pulled a leaf and turned it backside foremost, as the woman had said. 'I want a man,' she said; and sure enough the following spring she was wed again.

So she tried another leaf. 'I want a child,' she said; and she got a fine male bairn. 'What about a white stone house?' was her next request; and right enough she got it, and scrubbed it diligently.

Well, you'd think that would satisfy any woman, but no, she went haywire altogether and wished for combs, ornaments, trinkets and the like nonsense without success. These were not 'ideas'. So she took a tumble to herself and wished for hens, and she got them and worked for them; and she wished for kale and she found it; and she wished for lobsters and her husband got them for her, and as she ate one after another a voice in the wind said, 'Greedy, greedy!' So she sold them and made a profit.

Then one day she wished that she could have a whisky still, so that her husband could run it for her. Well, through time she got that too. But alas and alack, the both of them took to the drink, and there was no one left but the young man-child to tell the tale, as I am telling it to you . . .

The Gentle Art

Alexandrina's people had been weavers and spinners for several generations. Now it was traditional in those days in the Islands for the oldest daughter to inherit the spinning wheel and learn to use it; and this Alexandrina did quite willingly to the exclusion of all other maidenly activities like baking, churning, sewing, etc – not that she wanted to avoid the heavier work at all – it was just that the wheel itself fascinated her and had a very strange effect on her, a sort of hypnotic power. It could make her do almost anything. As she watched it going round and round she would start dreaming, and after a time she began experimenting secretly, confiding in the wheel, telling it what she wanted to do and seeing if it could make her do it. And it could! It could make her do anything. 'Teach me to waltz . . . waltz . . . waltz,' she would chant, and gradually she would leave the wheel and start dancing round the room like a spinning-top or a snowflake in a storm; then suddenly she would come to and feel lost and depressed. 'Teach me to bake, bake, bake,' and it did, and she would turn out the most amazing bannocks. And the strange thing is, these things she could never have done of her own accord – it needed the wheel to start her off.

Well, one fine autumn day as she sat at her wheel, the light and shadows singing through the spokes, it came to her suddenly that what she really wanted more than anything else in the world was a husband. She was shy at first about putting the likes of this to the wheel, and she had better be very careful as to which fellow she had in mind when she put the wheel in motion. Of course it would have to be Eachann, he was the one for her.

With extreme delicacy she fed and coaxed the wool, as the wheel went round, and hummed out her request,

> 'Eachann for me
> Och-ho och-he
> Give us your blessing
> And so let it be.'

And not too surprisingly, the very next day she found herself lifting potatoes shoulder to shoulder with her dream boy, and as they were lifting the third row he was asking if she could make butter. 'Oh yes,' she lied eagerly, knowing fine the wheel would help her.

'And can you bake, wash and sing?'

'Of course,' said Alexandrina.

'No man could ask for a better wife,' said Eachann, lifting the last plucean and rubbing the soil off his hands with his jumper to give her a splosher.

And by the time the shaws had flowered and withered that same summer they were wed. And there was nothing to mar their happiness except the spinning wheel. For Eachann was no fool and by degrees he guessed at the hold the wheel had on his wife: she was peddling away at the blooming thing morning, noon and night, and without knowing why, Eachann began to be jealous – so much so that one night when he asked her to cook a hare for his supper and she said, 'Wait a minute till I spin this bit yarn,' he lost his temper altogether and kicked the wheel to kingdom come – and that was disastrous.

There was no hare soup that night . . . nor was there any baking, singing or sewing in the days to follow, as Alexandrina had lost the art. Eachann called her an old witch who had deceived him and, sad to say, without the spinning wheel their marriage went on the rocks, and there was nothing that Alexandrina could do but seek the refuge of her mother's home. For hours she would wander about, staring with tear-washed eyes at the mountains that seemed to criss-cross like bootlaces over the cleft in the valley, till one day she met an old cailleach bringing home the peats, and she stopped to pass the time of day.

'What are you doing sitting here all alone, a young wife like you? Have you no man to go home to or no weans to feed?'

'No,' said Alexandrina, as she burst into floods of tears.

'Now, now, you'll be the better of that. Just you tell me all about it,' said the cailleach, and Alexandrina was only too glad to confide in someone outside the family. 'Well, you can stop that blubbering straightaway,' said the cailleach, 'for all you need is more confidence.'

'Gu dé rud a tha sin,' said Alexandrina in the Gaelic (meaning, 'What the heck is that?').

'Confidence, my dear, means learning to fend for yourself without looking for advice or help from anyone or anything. Come with me now and I'll teach you myself!'

And the little old woman took her back to her cottage, and in no time at all Alexandrina had learned to do all those things (even the singing) that meant so much to Eachann; and when she went back to him a far better woman, she found that he had become a far better man, for he'd missed her something terrible and had even repaired the spinning wheel – in the hope that she might some day come back to him – but of course she no longer needed that. And in due course Alexandrina handed it down to Dolina, her own first-born, for better or for worse.

The Kittens

My grandmother had a housekeeper once, Katie was her name, and she had a penfriend that she affectionately called a 'bosom pal'. She would sit by the kitchen fire and write long letters to her, and get even longer ones back. The postmark was Easter Dunfallandy, somewhere near Pitlochry I think it was, and Katie's bosom friend was in service there, house-keeper to a wealthy old skinflint who had promised to leave her something in his will; and although the money was poor the gentleman was in his eighties and getting very frail. He wasn't exactly in his dotage, mind you, just a little eccentric.

For instance, if you asked him the time of day he would say, politely enough, 'Half past the tail of my shirt and getting on for my trousers'; and if she said, 'how would you like your eggs boiled?' he'd say 'in water'. So Katie's friend Seonaid was not altogether surprised when he died and bequeathed her the cat and any kittens it might have in the future, instead of a reasonable sum of money.

Poor Seonaid didn't even have the price of her fare home. She was at her wits' end. 'The cat indeed, a fat bit of use that was.' Seonaid shooshed it impatiently out of her way, and started to pack her few belongings. Towards evening she was ready to leave, and looked for the cat to take it with her; after all, she had grown quite fond of the brute. 'Pushag, pushag,' she called, and then went out to look for it. The night was drawing in fast, she thought, and she had a mighty long walk ahead of her.

Just then she thought she heard mewing coming from the wild pear tree, and, as she approached, the mewing got louder but there wasn't a sign of the blooming cat. She started shaking the branches and it was then that she noticed a big hole in the trunk. She put her hand gingerly inside and pulled out a little piebald kitten, then another and another. Six in all! She shoved her sleeve up to the elbow and felt around for some more and her fingers touched what felt like a leather bag. It was quite heavy, and when she finally got it open she found to her amazement that it contained thirty golden sovereigns. So maybe the old man wasn't quite so daft after all . . .

Macleod's Maidens

A lot of people thought that young Archie was touched or moonstruck, which is not altogether surprising, as his poor mother was definitely off the beam. The poor woman is dead now. She died of tuberculosis some years ago when Archie was still a small child; so that was when young Archie was sent to live with his mother's two sisters. The three sisters had been known as the 'Macleod maidens', since they had lived all this time in a place called Fiscavaig, not far from the three magic outcrops of rock of that name.

Now these three sisters were very different from one another. The oldest was tall and lean and ugly, and the middle one was not so bad if left alone, but she was dominated by the eldest. Archie's mother, however, was completely different from the other two. Some say it was they who caused her to go into a decline, because she was always delicate and sensitive and, worst crime of all, she was pretty. She had also married a fine, handsome, able-bodied seaman and had a comfortable home, well-furnished by her husband who had brought to the marriage an heirloom in the shape of a magnificent antique grandfather clock. All these luxuries incensed the old girls, they were so jealous, and they reduced their young sister to a nervous wreck so much that she was afraid to go out in the daytime lest she should meet them and be harassed and criticised. So she took to going out at night, especially when there was a full moon, wheeling the pram with the infant Archie for miles. So it was no wonder that she went into a decline and died, and poor Archie had to go and live with the aunts together with his mother's furniture and effects, including the grandfather clock.

However, it so happened that the clock would not fit into the aunts' cottage and had to be put in the barn together with himself, the dog and the cow; because now that the old girls had got their hands on Archie's inheritance they became more greedy and worldly than ever and started taking in boarders and doing Bed and Breakfast, so there was no room for Archie. And as time went on they resented him more and more, after feeding him on leftover potato mash in the same dish with the dog. He often fell asleep cold and miserable in the barn, wishing he could be away.

And this eventually he did, getting work at the prawn fishing and working hard trying to put a bit aside so that one day he could have his own boat – but he found it wasn't at all easy to save with so many temptations in places like Stornoway. What with drams with the men, tee shirts and fine shoes and chickens on the grill, there was never anything left; and when the fishing stopped in the winter he was broke and forced back home to the misery and the abuse of his aunties.

So, skulking in the barn one night his attention was drawn to the grandfather clock, and he got a bright idea. The mechanism and works were all rusted now, so why should he not gut it out, line it with cement and make a boat of it? The weights would be for ballast and he could make oars from parts of the casing. So he got to work through the winter nights, and by the early spring had fashioned himself a fine craft. Then, by the light of the full moon, without a word to anyone, he shoved the boat down to the sea and launched it. He got in and, rowing himself a mile or two out he felt fairly confident, when suddenly the wind got up and the rain came down in torrents and here, didn't he find that he could not bale out fast enough and the boat was sinking fast, lower and lower in the water; and he began to pray and to panic and he was sure he was going to drown, when suddenly he realised there was a great big fish's fin hooking on to the gunwale on the port side of the boat. Quickly he leaned over to grab it but there was no need, as the great tail of an enormous fish began to slither backside foremost into the boat; and at the other end of it it wasn't a fish's head at all but a beautiful woman, marvellously formed, with glorious red-gold hair right down to her navel, and he was so astonished he didn't know what to say or what to do.

Then she said to him, 'Don't you be afraid of me, Archie, I won't harm you. I know all about you since the day you were born, and your poor mother also with her tuberculosis and her coughing and her bad chest, and how she couldn't sleep at night and would get up and put you in the pram and push you out along the road in the moonlight; and she would put prayers up to the full moon asking that you would not become afflicted like her but would grow up a fine man, strong and healthy, and this you certainly are and handsome into the bargain. And I know all about these two terrible aunties of yours and how they ill-treat you, and I don't want you to continue living there any more, so am now going to give you the kiss of everlasting life so that you won't drown in this storm, as you would have if I hadn't come along in the nick of time, dear Archie!'

So with that she reached out and curled her long arms round his neck, bending him back and kissing him in the most extraordinary way, saying that that would give him everlasting life and that he would now be able to come down with her into the bottom of the ocean where he would remain in the prime of his life for ever, and in the height of comfort and the lap of luxury. And with that she gave an almighty bash to the side of the boat with her tail and capsized it, then grabbed ahold of Archie and down, down, down they both went to the very bottom of the ocean.

At the bottom here was an enormous black cave all lit up inside with phosphorescence; starfish hung from the roof of it, glinting and sparkling, and there were gigantic, comfortable-looking couches made from sponges, and tables and chairs. There were fishnet curtains, a microwave, deep freeze, washing machine with automatic hot geyser rinse attached, ice-cream cones galore (real shell ones), everything in fact that a man could possibly wish for. And she was showing him such favours – enough to make a fellow blush – but he got used to it! He was feeling stronger and healthier, completely relaxed and content; and through time they had a lot of little fishes and some of them looked exactly like himself – a quite remarkable achievement one would have thought.

There are of course a lot of stories connected with the *Macleod Maidens* . . . the most common being that three glamorous sisters from the Outer Hebrides had been promised in marriage to three of Macleod's kinsmen. They were all of noble birth and a great feast was arranged for the arrival of the brides-to-be. They were betrothed by remote control, gentlemen's agreements, barter for cattle and arms, or maybe some sort of part exchange – who knows, but anyway they were due to arrive in Skye when the weather changed and a ninety-mile-an-hour hurricane-gale was imminent. The Minch was churning up great waves and there was no way the men on shore could get a line to the ill-fated boat; it was lifted like matchwood right out of the water, and flung onto the rocks not far from Dunvegan Head – a beautiful place called Fiscavaig. It's a beautiful name and an even more beautiful place.

If you stand on a hillock amongst the long whispering grass of the marshes on a summer's day and look down below you to the pink blushing, lobster-coloured beach with tide-marking all over it like the furrows on an old man's brow; then look beyond that again to the pancake-like blue-green islands scattered here and there like a child's bricks; then look further still again as far as the eye can see and there, my goodness, stand the three magical outcrops of rock, the tallest one shaped like a bell, the middle one squatting as though sitting down, and the little one crouched at the end as though in obeisance to the other two. And these are the three *Macleod Maidens*, – and there I hope they will stay for all eternity. And I have no doubt that the aforesaid three young suitors would drown their sorrows in the only way they knew how, and believe that through time they would find con-solation in the arms of other maidens. But they would always be reminded, as we are, that we can never look across at all those magnificent rocks, petrified for the rest of eternity, without heaving a sigh of regret.

Of course I have got my own notion of how these rocks were named . . . it must have been way back before time began. It is well known that the islands had not got Christianity until quite late on, and before that they were moon worshippers.

At the time of the full moon the people, young and old, would scramble out of their half-submerged dwellings and rush down to the eclipse of the tide with its ladders of light glinting over and upwards to the darkening heavens. Now was the time to dance, now was the birth of the Highland reel and a great ho-ro gheallaidh was in fact had by all.

Ho-ro a'ghealach ag éirigh
A'ghealach ag éirigh
A'ghealach ag éirigh
Tiugainn a mach
A'ghealach ag éirigh!

'Ho-ro a'ghealach ag éirigh' means 'ho-ro the moon is rising', because 'a'ghealach' is the Gaelic for white moon.

They would also make sacrifices to the moon, and it is not beyond the bounds of possibility that young virgins, young beautiful maidens, were not infrequently sacrificed to the moon – and it is my opinion that the men were probably Macleods for they are not all the stalwart heroes they are cracked up to be by a long chalk, and some of them were quite despicable in what they attempted to do. They were very good for instance at flinging their wives into dungeons, feeding them with salt meat, denying them water, poking their eyes out and God knows what – so it is more than likely that they might well have taken these Macleod Maidens and tied them up onto the rocks there at Fiscavaig and waited till the tide came in to sacrifice them to the moon; then they would dance and yell and shout and no doubt have a good dram to celebrate the occasion.

It could be, on the other hand, they could just be tied there for commercial reasons in the same way as the African slaves were chained down on the docks in Liverpool to be shipped off to America. It's not too far out to believe that these three Macleod Maidens might well have been tied there until the fishing fleet came in from Spain or Germany or anywhere in fact; and possibly one would be taken aback to sail off to Nova Scotia, and another maybe to New Zealand with the sheep – and you know, the wee pretty one might just have been dropped off at Mallaig to become a fish gutter; but that's just a theory – so you can make of it what you will.

The Corn Cailleach

This yarn I want to spin was told to me by my grandmother. I am called after my grandmother, therefore I will take the liberty of using her name (God rest her soul). I am Nighean Mairianna Beathag (the daughter of my mother and grandmother, in the Gaelic). You see, my married name is completely unpronounceable except by my husband himself!

I think of my grandmother a lot, and the hard life she had raising ten children and God knows how many grandchildren. The outside work must have been the hardest; she was in fact, cutting the corn when my mother was born. That's why my mother had two birthdays, one at the end of the harvest time (mid-September) and one in November, when my grandfather got home from sea to register the birth.

Nevertheless, the average crofter's wife was a strong healthy woman, must have been, since it was not unknown for her to actually give birth to a child in the field and carry on working just as though nothing had happened. You see, the corn was very precious, and a good crop would mean a great deal of rejoicing and merrymaking, and they would cut it to the very last few straws which were known in many parts of the Scottish Highlands and Islands as 'a'Chailleach' (the old woman), and these they would preserve.

It is most astonishing how a mouse or a hare or a weasel can hide out in a vast field of the stuff, and only scuttle when the last small patch is about to be cut. In ancient times these animals were believed to harbour evil spirits, and effigies were made of straw representing them. These would be burnt, usually on a hill or mountainside away from the village and the people running away from the flames would shout, 'The De'il will tak the hindmost, slàinte!' And 'De'il tak the hindmost' (or slowest drinker) is a toast till this very day.

In some foreign places, Poland for instance, a fair maiden is chosen to cut the last patch, and a crown is made from it interwoven with flowers and coloured ribbons. And it is not unknown in Scotland for straw hares and dolls to be made and kept a year for luck. Sometimes they would just hang the last of the crop above the living-room door like a Catholic icon or Jewish scroll.

Skye's The Limit

For as long as I can remember we had spent part of the year in Skye with my grandmother, usually the summer part when her garden smelt so wonderful it made you want to cry. At the foot of it there was a hedge of fuschia sheltering it from the very edge of the sea. The shore was so near that the plants we threw out took root amongst the rocks and shells, especially montbretia. If you make a split in a montbretia leaf and shove the pointed end in the slot, it makes a wonderful boat – keel and all – but you probably know that.

I loved my grandmother's house* better than anywhere else in the world, and it was to become our permanent home up until World War II. Nobody thought of war in those days, except my grandmother's generation. She had lost four sons in the first war. But that was not unusual. All the women her age had lost sons in that war. There were photographs hanging in every home of men with white spats, glengarries and hairy sporrans.

In the evenings there would be stories of heroes who had left the island by the gig-load, and sad eerie tales told by peat flame, candle and lamplight. But these were not told on

* The house is down on the shore road opposite the jetty (Broadford), that was where we lived. Tigh an Liubhrais (Liveras House) was only a five-bedroom house, bathroom, kitchen and maid's room.

summer nights. In fact there was no night at all in summer, only the Northern Lights and the burning of the heather on the mountainsides, and the sound of the bagpipes far off across the water at some céilidh or dance.

I would wake in the mornings to the penetrating English voice of my father shouting, 'Hurry up if you're coming, girl! The tide's going out and the steamer will be here soon. The place will be infested with tourists. Damn it. Who's been cutting these roses on the veranda again?'

The smell of roses and catmint was intoxicating. I rolled out of my silver-painted bed onto the purple carpet and moved towards the window. I could see the old paddle steamer making its way from Portree, and Angus Donald the carrier rattling down the pier to meet it. 'Won't be a minute,' I called in a weak voice.

I wanted to sound remote, ethereal, like Camille, the Lady of the Camellias. I'd painted my room to suit my mood only the other day. Taking a look at myself in the long mirror I turned sideways (I looked more frail that way, fragile, more consumptive). Perhaps I should stop getting suntanned? Camille would never have had a tan. Big Cameron, newly retired from South Africa, had invested his money in a travelling cinema and had shown the excellent film by Alexander Dumas in the church hall. I had still not recovered.

My father yelled, 'Come on, come on!'

Men! I wriggled my thin body into the bathing costume my mother had just finished knitting for me, and nearly wept. The stitches were far too loose, and one wee nipple was smiling back at me from the mirror. Well, it would have to do. The tide was going out, there was no time to lose.

Nearly sixty, my father was still a wonderful swimmer. He dived off the old pier every morning from May till September and came to be known as 'Bodach na Mara' (Old Man of the Sea). I went with him most days, tumbling in off the third-lowest step, gulping the salt water and fighting for survival in those ice-cold Atlantic seas, only fit for men and mermaids.

Once I was stung by an inkfish. It swam under my body and reached out its yard-long tentacles, enveloping me. Father came to my rescue and brought me home on Angus Donald's cart, all wrapped up in flour sacks. 'Keep her down in a bath of boiling water till the tide turns,' he said. And this legend was true; the wee doctor confirmed it. 'The moment the tide turns the pain will go, not before! Mind you, she'll never know what it is to have rheumatism now,' he said. And I never have.

Most mornings Paddy Craig the poacher would be down on the shore counting his catch from the night before. 'Here's a couple of trout for your breakfast,' said Paddy, 'and don't let the new laird' (Captain Shaw) 'catch you. I sent him an anonymous gift of a stag's head not so long ago. I wouldn't want him to put two and two together. Will you be at the dance tonight? There's one in Heaste. I'll give you a lift over.'

'Not on your Nellie,' and I would race back to the house concealing the loose-knit swimsuit with fish and towel, as best I could.

After breakfast, (porridge and cream, fried trout, and ham and eggs) I lay on my back on the old church pew at the side of the house at Liubhrais. Liubhrais meant 'a bridle path' in Gaelic (where the horses came along), or sort of fairy track. I speculated about that as I lay there in the hot sun on this early June morning, thinking how lucky I was to get a good stretch with no one seeing me.

I moved my hand lazily along the edge of the warm wood of the old church pew. A thundering great splinter got into it. Pulling it out with my teeth I wondered if perhaps there was a spell, or buidseachd, on the pew. Was a pew a holy thing? Would it not have been better to leave it in the church where it had always been, instead of the shiny new yellow ones my uncle had donated? I wriggled my bare toes and laughed out loud . . . At the sale my mother had been bidding against herself. She had forgotten that she had asked Paddy Craig to get a pew for her, and started bidding. The price just soared higher and higher. Even the undertaker couldn't keep pace. Church pews would be invaluable to him to make the sides of the coffins. It would cut down his expenses a lot . . .

From the corner of one eye I could see my grandmother who had come out to gather blackcurrants for her excellent jams. She reminded me of the sketches by Boz in the Charles Dickens' volumes my father had bought for us. (It didn't occur to me that she looked in any way silly in the numerous black silk skirts she wore.) Her black shiny hair, parted in the middle, was in sharp contrast to her white skin and still whiter mutch, or currac (a sort of frail muslin bonnet with large white ties under the chin). I was called after her and therefore considered it a privilege to sit for hours holding the goffering-iron while her beautiful Mackinnon hands moved up and down, round the edge of her muslin currac. She too could sit for hours, fingers entwined, rotating her thumbs first one way and then the other, her low-pitched voice humming a mysterious haunting Gaelic rune or melody.

Horses were bad luck to *her*, and to all her clan; to dream of them foretold a death in the family. One of her sons had been thrown and the tinkers had carried him home in very bad shape. They hadn't stolen his horse, though. She never turned them away from her door after that. There wasn't much opportunity for riding in Skye.

Once I had been left behind when the whole family had taken every available means of transport and gone to the games at Kyleakin. They were going to stay overnight. I stayed up sulking and at five in the morning I walked to Achadh a' Chùirn (the Field of Corn Stacks) where my Uncle Neil lived. Neilag would never refuse to let me have his horse. He would never refuse me anything; I reminded him of a sweetheart he once had in Spain when he'd roamed the seven seas. Indeed, he got his wife up at that hour to make some fudge (knowing I had a sweet tooth). We ate it till we were sick, while he sat and entertained me with stories, in his boots and semmit and drawers (or long johns), puffing away at his pipe and recounting the time when, as a young man, he'd broken ship and been chased by a seven-foot nigger, who had put him in irons and flung him in jail; and how he'd got out wearing the railings away with a brick from the wall (or was it his teeth?). He was only really stalling for time. He completed his dressing and, round about eleven, went out to saddle the horse for me. Not being much of an agriculturalist I didn't know wheat from barley, let alone barley from clover. He'd deliberately put the hungry horse in a field of the stuff and, short of massacring the beast, I was unable to make it move. I sat there twigging the reins, cudgelling and beseeching till the late afternoon, with Neilag hiding behind a peatstack killing himself with laughter.

There is nothing quite like cantering along on a fine horse through scenery second to none, a wild wind tugging at the roots of your hair, the sharp cut line of the Cuillins showing through the clouds, the warm slopes of Blàbheinn, and the rings of morning smoke curling up from the cottages to meet the mountain haze.

What was in this air that gushed through the gullies creating music, whispering words, filling the imagination for centuries past? Samuel Johnson had been inspired by Corry and Elgol. Mrs Pankhurst's sister was unable to tear herself away from the place. Today's children born at the foot of these mountains were to become, in the future, top models, politicians and authors – notorious if not famous – at home and abroad. I waved to a girl my own age in bare feet and carrying her boots slung on her shoulder, who would become masseuse to the Duke of Kent and Princess Marina. I had already passed a lad who would marry the Prime Minister's daughter. And none of them knew their fate!

Dismounting and entering a cottage I was greeted by a man in a sailor's jersey, the name of his ship written across his back, and wearing army boots. 'Will you wait for the dance tonight?' he said. 'The blind fiddler will be there . . . and we all know how fond you are of him.'

'Will he have his Stradivarius?'

'Ach, it's no a joke!' said the tall man. 'It is a Stradivarius and he wouldn't part with it for all the money in the world. It's been here since Fear a' Choire* himself entertained Johnson and Boswell so lavishly. Man! Those were the days! The women with silk dresses all the way from Spain, and the

* Fear a' Choire – the laird of Corry, Mackinnon. The ruin is there where the guests stayed off the Torrin Road.

men with more drink in them than there are waters in Coruisk.'

I accepted a plate of mealy potatoes* and herring which we washed down with a bowl of buttermilk, then departed for home. I would have to go past the Cill Chriosd Loch and the cemetery where all my ancestors were buried. It was getting late. The marble quarry, too, was spooky as hell. Lights flashing off and on and unseen hands tugging at your clothes was a common occurrence, and no wonder. Roughly a century ago two men celebrating at a wedding had gone out for air. They were both in love with the same girl. They had walked towards the loch and an hour later one of them came back, panting, his clothes all torn and wet and his face as white as a sheet. 'He's gone,' he shouted. 'He's gone . . .' Each Uisge, the water horse got him by the hair and dragged him down into the loch with its big white flashing teeth.

They fully believed his story and nothing more was done about it. But there is a buidseachd on that man's family till this very day, so my grandmother says.

My grandmother was such a novelty, she was different from other people. People were becoming modern and wearing modern clothes by this time, by the time I was seven anyway. And my mother was always extremely smart, she had great taste in clothes and lovely hats and things, she was a good-looking woman. And there was my grandmother with her currac and her five long petticoats, one cotton, one silk, one of red flannel and another one stripes and another of black. Oh yes, she wore them all at once! And then wee corsets high up that pushed her bosom up to her chin, and

* mealy potatoes – soft and dry, cooked with heavy skins on

they were laced tight tight tight! She would ask me sometimes to lace them for her. And she was so meticulous about
her dressing, amazing for a peasant woman. But she had
lovely wee wee feet and square-toed shoes, immaculately
polished. One thing she did have was lovely hands, that's the
Mackinnon hands, it's not MacLeod hands at all. They were
weavers; unlike the MacLeods they were more artistic,
dreamers, and they cared for their hands and didn't work
so hard . . . They were making things from the beginning of
time.*

* After my grandmother, Rebekah Mackinnon, I was christened
Rebecca Mary Sykes. My great-grandmother was also Rebecca and
came from the back of the Island of Scalpay, where her mother,
also Rebecca, had lived and is reputed to have been spinning yarn
for her trousseau when a boatload of men from Raasay came and
kidnapped her (see 'Consider an Island' above). I gave the remains
of the wheel to my brother's grandchild Rebecca Hughes in the
hope that she too will hand it down to a Rebecca with my love (see
illustration).

The Laundry Maid

Distant thunder made me hurry along, then came two large drops of rain on the back of my hand, and streaks of lightning in the sky, and I decided to run for it until I reached the old laundry. Anything less like a laundry you couldn't imagine. It was more like an old tumble-down cottage with a magnificent corrugated, bright scarletty-orange roof, all worn away at the edges like a burnt rice pudding. It was quite enchanting and a good place to shelter in. So I leaned against the rotting lintel of the doorway.

There were already bits of grass and corn growing out of the rotten wood and even a little tree pushing its way. I was very intrigued with the place. I loved it dearly and often came this way. It seemed absurd, but it was built at least a quarter of a mile away from the mansion itself and had always been known as the laundry, because at one time it had contained two great big porcelain ironstone sinks and, believe it or not, outside the doorway was the most enchanting iron pump you ever saw! True Victoriana. It would fetch a bomb* if it was taken to one of the salerooms in London. It had a long iron handle, was tall and had an ornate cap on the top of it. I was fascinated with it and the whole place – the great eighteen-inch thick walls filled with moss here and there and such

* fetch a bomb – make you rich (Sl)

beautiful colours the stones had acquired – white, yellow, a painter's dream in fact. I stood there for a long time remembering stories I had heard about the place. One in particular about a little laundry maid called Seonaid.

She was but a slip of a girl with raven black hair and blue eyes and a skin just like milk. The mind boggles how she reached the great porcelain sinks – never mind minding the wheel of the huge, giant mangle – and using the pump of course was out of the question. But in those days the laird employed at least sixteen servants and they were all very, very fond of little Seonaid and she was never allowed to do anything beyond her strength. She would far rather draw water from the river than try to work the great iron stoup, but the gemmer who was about her own age was always very willing to help her – and it wasn't all work in those days for this laird was a generous man and lenient into the bargain, and he used to bring all his friends, many of whom were talented, up from London after the holiday season was over. He would bring them up North for his house parties. He would put on games and charades and all kinds of amusements for them, and they would have wonderful parties and he was equally good for those below the sale. He would organise dances and céilidhs in the barns for his staff, which as I said was numerous.

Now one of these nights there was a party going on in the big house with very important guests including the laird's mother-in-law, the old dowager, who was well known for enjoying a party very much indeed. In fact she was over-fond of her port and would very often have to be sent off to bed halfway through the evening.

This particular evening there was also a great horoghealaidh, or party, going on in the barn for the staff. They were all having a wild and hilarious time and they were all there except for Seonaid and one or two other maids. So in the big house when the dowager suddenly collapsed, having indulged herself overmuch – and indeed vomited all over her beautiful silken matinée coat – Seonaid was sent for to take the coat away to the laundry and have it cleaned on the following day, as it was now nearing midnight. So Seonaid eased the jacket off the swooning dowager and made her way in the dark of the night towards the laundry. The smell of the jacket was nauseating to her because as I said she was a feeble and delicate young girl and very beautiful. So when she got to the river which ran alongside the old laundry she decided that she would dook the jacket in the river to get rid of the smell and the worst of the vomit; but she couldn't help laughing when she remembered the story her mother had once told her about a man in the north end of Skye who had many children – six I think it was – and he never did a day's work in his life and he was an absolute drunk. He would go off and get drunk as a cow every evening and when he got home his starving children would dance around him calling out and pleading with him, 'Please, Daddy, sick big bits, sick big bits,' they were that hungry. So Seonaid had a good giggle to herself because perhaps the story wasn't quite true. And she made her way on till she reached the laundry, and left the jacket there and went back to join the others at the party in the barn.

It took the old dowager all the next day to get rid of her hangover and pull herself together. She was, you know, rather senile. 'Where are my teeth?' she spluttered. 'Where are my teeth? Oh God, where is my necklace, where is my necklace? Oh dear me, who put me to bed? Who undressed me?' And so Seonaid was sent for and brought before her ladyship. 'What did you do with my clothes? What did you do with my things?'

And Seonaid said, 'Well, I put them all neatly away and your matinée jacket I took down to the laundry to be laundered for you. I didn't do it myself, but it has been laundered and it is now here ready for you to wear again this evening if you should so wish, my lady.'

'Yes,' said she, 'but what about my teeth and my necklace? What have you done with them?'

'Oh dear me,' said Seonaid, 'I haven't seen anything like that. I never saw any teeth or necklaces at all, just the jacket.'

'You're a liar,' piped the old senile woman. 'You know perfectly well you must have done something with them' – and she called all the staff in to search and search her room and her drawers and her wardrobe and everything – and it was astonishing the amount of aniseed that fell out of her wardrobe and old empty port-wine bottles as well, but there certainly was no sign of teeth or the necklace that she maintained she had been wearing. Of course the laird himself had noticed that she was wearing a lovely necklace, because it was he himself who had given it to her for her eighty-seventh birthday.

So as Seonaid was the last to be with her before she collapsed entirely the previous night, she was questioned and questioned, and in the end she was accused of theft; and in those days if a woman was accused of theft she was invariably sent to Glasgow and to jail, and this indeed is what happened to the poor, unfortunate Seonaid. She was sent off to Glasgow and put in prison.

Mind you, the laird who had been fond of the girl didn't believe for one minute that she was guilty of theft, and so he very promptly sent enough money for her release. He put up bail in other words. But Seonaid could not bring herself to go back to her home; there was no way she could go and face all these people who had accused her because she knew in her heart that she was totally innocent; she had never set eyes on the missing teeth or necklace. And so she went and called at a labour exchange and finally got herself a job on the outskirts of Glasgow on a farm, a dairy farm, and her job was to be delivering the milk around the suburbs of Glasgow. She did this together with the farmer's son.

They would both set out at the crack of dawn, five-thirty in the morning, with a cart, a milk-float driven by a horse. It was great fun; she enjoyed it enormously and it wasn't a heavy job either. All she had to do was to ladle the milk into little galvanised buckets with lids on and deliver them round the doors. The horse and Johnny the farmer's son would follow behind her, and Johnny and she became very good friends. They went to the cinema together and they went to dances together and gradually Seonaid became more herself again, and eventually they got married.

Now I would never have been able to complete this story if I hadn't gone into the laundry to shelter from the rain, and my curiosity drove me to go further into the interior of the old place. And by so doing I disturbed a bird in a nest up in the rafters and it became so agitated it started to fly round and round and round. It struck me once or twice but it wasn't in an unfriendly sort of way. I had the feeling that it wanted to caress me. I felt a weird sensation of arms folding around me and when its wing brushed my cheek it felt like a kiss and then, to my astonishment, as the bird flew frenziedly round and round, all about, striking the wall here and striking the wall there suddenly the old mangle creaked into action. The great iron wheel started to turn all by itself and a crackling sound came from the little fireplace underneath the boiler. And then, eerily, I heard the handle of the pump going up and down and up and down and water began to flow into the sink. The strange thing was I wasn't at all frightened. Weird shadows moved backwards and forwards and then I heard a voice saying in Gaelic, '*Cha robh fios agam*, I knew not where it was, I knew not where it was.' Then everything went silent, deadly silent, and I realised I had experienced a telling, not uncommon in these parts . . .

I heard of a woman in the north end of Skye who one day, sitting by the fire, heard the chairs in the room around her starting to clank together and then outside her door she heard the sound of hymns being sung and the voices of many people. A week later her husband died, there was a funeral and the chairs were put outside to make a trestle on which to rest the coffin, and the minister led the singing in all the Gaelic hymns. This is what she had heard in advance of his death.

I drew in my breath and wondered what all this could mean to me. What was I supposed to do? I was being told by Seonaid that she hadn't stolen anything, so surely it was my duty to get out of here as quickly as possible and go up to the big house and tell them what I had heard. They were related to me anyway.

So I asked to speak to the laird and he was very gracious and took me into the morning room and ordered coffee. And I sat in a big old winged chair by the window; the room was sunny and bright and lined with books, and he said, 'Well, it's lovely to see you, what have you got to say for yourself these days, my dear?'

And I told him I had been down to visit the old laundry which had always fascinated me. 'What are you going to do about that place?' I said. 'It is really too beautiful to waste.'

'Oh,' he said, 'I am not going to be doing anything with it at all. It saddens me when I look at it nowadays.'

'Well,' I said, 'I am going to tell you an extraordinary thing. I had a message from Seonaid in it. I heard her voice and she was telling me that she was not guilty of the theft of the necklace.'

'I know,' said the laird, 'I know quite well, and oh my God I feel so guilty. You see I was walking along one day about a month ago, and I had the dogs with me and I let them loose into the river and one of them, big Fanny here, she came dashing out of the water. I was wearing the kilt and she splattered me all over, wet my kilt and wet my knees, and I was very irritated and then of all things she opened her gob and dropped a pair of false teeth at my feet. I couldn't believe my eyes and then she regurgitated and produced the necklace. I was absolutely astonished and mortified and wondered how on earth this could possibly have happened. I found the address of Seonaid through the farm she had been working at in Glasgow and I sent a cable to Canada asking her to forgive us all and come back if she possibly could, that her job would be waiting here for her or she could be compensated. I was willing to compensate her for all the shame I had brought upon her. And I learned with shame and mortification, and Seonaid had gone slowly into decline and had often moaned and groaned and wished that she could be back home in Skye where she belonged, and her husband wanted no compensation from me or anyone else and swore that he would never forgive me or my clan for the injustice we had shown his wife.

'I spent endless time questioning the dowager who had at long last confessed she remembered now, that when she began to feel sick that night she had been afraid of losing her teeth, and had taken them out and taken the necklace herself off her neck and put them in an inside pocket in the lining of her matinée jacket, and had forgotten all about it. "Seonaid, when she was taking it to the laundry so late at night and in the dark," she concluded, "must have stumbled and dropped it in the river." It was obvious that the poor child knew nothing of what had happened to her jewellery and her teeth.

'It so happens the old trout, my mother-in-law, has passed on herself, and I am not really sorry for she had a tongue like a marline-spike and was far from honest. However, she did leave that necklace behind, and I think since you got the telling from Seonaid herself down at the laundry, I would like to fasten it round your neck as a present from me.'

Bandy Willie and the Dinner

There was a wee bandy-legged laddie living with his granny in Braes a long time ago and he wasn't exactly bright. Some said he was mach às a rian (out of his mind). He was always getting thrashings with the tawse at the school and by jove, the schoolmaster didn't hesitate to use it! 'Children couldn't have things all their own way,' he said.

And there was strict discipline in the church and home, too. If you wanted any shenanigans then you had to find them outside, somewhere where no one could see you. Well, that was all right through the week, there were lots of things you could do then: play up at the old sheep fank, hide under the bridges to frighten the girls on their way home from the school, catch fish in the burn with your bare hands, go o'er your wilkie* down the brae, or just aim at the telegraph cups with a stone and a catapult. But Sundays were different. You couldn't get out at all, except to go to church, and during the communion time you couldn't get out for part of the week either. Herds of white-faced, black-clad men and women would arrive from all over the place, from Plockton and Applecross and Kyle and wee Bandy Willie's granny always had an open house. She would sleep as many as six or seven cousins, some of

* o'er your wilkie – tumble head over heels (Sc)

them on shakedown on 'the room'* floor, and some of them squashing the guts out of themselves in the wee room above the kitchen. The food was always prepared in advance for the communion, and the smell of it would drive you up the wall, especially if you had a healthy young appetite.

Now young Bandy Willie had another affliction. Asthma it was called, and he couldn't sit through a long kirk session without getting an attack, so he was left at home in charge of the dinner. He had to put the pre-peeled potatoes on at the right time and keep stirring the stew or soup or whatever it was to be.

Well, this particular Sunday it was to be rabbit stew, and it smelt awful good. His granny had put it on to simmer, before she and her cousins went off to the communion service (peppermints an' all). They had left simple Willie in charge. Well now, any other boy would have found it hard to keep his fingers out of that stew, stirring it and licking the wooden spoon hour after hour. In the end Old Nick[†] got the better of him and persuaded him to take a sample of it; this he did, but it only whetted his appetite the more . . . and now he would stop at nothing. Before he knew it he had helped himself to far too much for it not to be missed.

Since he wasn't allowed out on the Sunday he couldn't catch another rabbit to replace his portion. Then it was his cunning little eyes spied the cat . . . and in his poor half-crazed mind there was no difference between snaring and skinning a rabbit, and snaring and skinning a cat. At any rate it made an ample addition to the stew, and when his granny

* the room – room kept immaculately clean, seldom used except for funerals, births, communion times or any special guests
[†] Old Nick – the Devil (Sc)

and her cousins all trooped in, starving with hunger and not a single peppermint left, they lost no time in putting up a scanty grace and getting stuck in to their food, which they ate with relish, complimenting Willie in an offhand but Godly sort of way, on his fine cooking.

It wasn't till the evening after the Good Book had been read, and they started to lock up and look for the cat . . . that they began to be suspicious. But they could never prove anything . . . could they? Since Willie had burnt the skin. And it tasted mighty like rabbit, true enough.

Silver Strands

There was a strange widow-woman once who lived in the north end of Skye . . . many years ago it was; she lived in Glen Hinnisdal, or, maybe it was Cuidrach, I couldn't be sure. Anyway, she was handsome enough to look at with her silver-grey hair which she wore in a big loose bundle at the back of her long neck. She reminded one of a seal – the sleekness of her and the smooth way she moved about with long, swinging strides. She had a smooth tongue in her head too. Some said she was sly and not to be trusted and a lot were afraid of her because they suspected her of practising the Black Art. They watched her, fascinated, as she went striding off to the peats with her creel, for on the way back she would stop to gather all sorts of herbs from the sides of the burns and jars of tadpoles and frogs from the loch. There was no doubt about it, she was a bit of a witch, and few people ever dared to visit her.

Now her son Alec was quite a different kettle of fish. They liked him fine, and he was handsome too in his own way – blond, lanky and lean, a little effeminate perhaps – but saved from being too pretty by having his nose bashed in while playing shinty, which as we all know is a real man's game. He was quite good company if the cailleach wasn't around. She, you see, had a strange power over him and would hardly let him out of her sight. From birth she had namby-pambied him something terrible, making him wear two semmits under the jersey and the thickest stockings bulging out of his boots that you ever saw in your life. She knitted them all herself, spinning the coarse wool that she found on the fences and dykes. And here's a strange thing: into every pair of stockings that she knitted she wove several locks of her own silver-grey hair, not for warmth or decoration, but because it gave her a special magic power over him, a sort of contact; she could communicate and influence him; she had got the tabs on him, so to speak, good and proper. So great was her selfish frustration that she did everything she could think of not to let go of her son. She had lost one man in her life and by hook or by crook, or by her own form of black magic, she would keep this one at her side for ever.

But young Alec had other ideas and he was fed up with his mother always cramping them, and he was particularly fed up with those blooming stockings that she made him wear. He was the laughing-stock of the place, and so he took to taking them off and hiding them in the ditch till he was ready to go home again. In this way he discovered that he felt much freer and more himself, and in this way, running about barefooted and wild as a bird, he met Raonaid. Raonaid, whose eyes were purple and hair the colour of peat. He was in love with her from the very first day he met her – the day she said, 'I'm going to take off my stockings too, and I'll race you to the bottom of the bealach.' That was him sunk.

When he was old enough to court her properly and the time would grow near of an evening for him to put on his boots and socks, that was the time when his mother's influence grabbed on to him again. So the moonlight was wasted, and Alec would start to say horrible things to his loved one – things like, 'Dhia, I don't know what I've been seeing in you all day – you're not a patch on Curstag Bhàn' (and poor Curstag Bhàn was a fat, skelly-eyed lump).

So Raonaid would begin to cry and Alec couldn't stand that anyway and so off he went, trundling down the croft in his hairy socks home to ma, leaving Raonaid to commune alone in the moonlight with the moan of the wind and the groan of the plunging Atlantic waves dashing themselves against the rocks to aggravate her mood of desolation. 'What came over him?' she wondered. 'It must be something to do with that old witch, his mother,' and she made up her mind to get to the bottom of it.

Now it so happened that Raonaid and her family had come over to Skye from the Outer Isles, where the women were famous for their weaving and knitting, and Raonaid herself was a dab hand at doing all the most difficult Fair Isle patterns. In fact, most of the women envied her skill, and some of them – shame to tell – her beauty. The most envious of all was Alec's mother: she had brought herself to hate the girl, and had started brewing up all sorts of magic potions and was turning over in her evil mind ways and means of poisoning her; and she would have succeeded too, no doubt, if Raonaid hadn't always taken great care to carry a hare's foot round with her and to wear a bunch of crimson rowan berries in her dark brown hair to ward off the evil spirits that she might encounter. She took all these precautions because she had every intention of calling on Alec's mother (she was a brave girl, indeed). She would take the bull by the horns, so to speak, and fight for her lover if need be. At any rate she wanted to see how the land lay.

So, early one evening when she knew Alec was helping at

the shearing she barged right into the old woman's kitchen, and caught her in the very act of clipping long strands off her grey hair and spinning it in with the yarn on the spinning wheel; so Raonaid guessed at once how it was that she had such a strong pull on poor Alec! However, she never let on that she had seen anything untoward (a Highland expression) and was very polite, pretending that she had come to borrow some purple wool to finish a Fair Isle pattern that she was in a hurry for.

'I haven't any wool to spare – purple or pink,' said the cailleach, 'and even if I had, you wouldn't get it; but if you wait a minute,' she added (changing her tune a bit), 'I can give you a drop of green soap to wash your bonny hair with.'

'What a two-faced old besom,' thought Raonaid – but she said, 'Thank you, that will be fine,' rather nervously. Then she watched her sneak off into a corner and concoct a jar of messy-looking stuff which Raonaid was quite sure would be three parts poison – and indeed she was right, for when she got home she tried a bit of it on the end of the cat's tail and the poor wee pushag was left naked and hairless as the face of the moon. And that's how Raonaid got the bright idea remembering the poem, 'Tit for tat, killed the cat . . .'

She got to work straightaway and made the prettiest bonnet, mutch, or currac you have ever seen in all your life – twenty-nine different colours in it and eighteen different patterns, and long silk ribbons to tie under the chin – and steeped the lot in a warm lather of the old witch's green soap all night long. Next day she paid a second visit. 'Here's a wee present for you,' she said, 'but you'll need to try it on first to see if the fit is right.'

Well, needless to say, the cailleach grabbed at the bonnet

without hesitation and pressed it well down on her head, and so taken up with herself was she that she wouldn't take it off again – and in fact, nor could she – for if she did she would be as bald as a turnip, and Alec would burst himself with laughing at her; for without her long grey hair she no longer had a power over him, or Raonaid for that matter, or any of the impudent wee grandchildren that came along in due course; for Raonaid and Alec were a very happy married couple, or so everyone used to say – everyone, that is, except . . . the poor old witch with the alopecia!!

The Lonely Ones

Sitting in front of the fire on one of those little stools with a slot in the middle like a letter box, Sheena stroked the cat purring away on her knees.* She loved the sound of the purr, it closed her off from the rest of the world. She liked that. Sometimes she would get up and turn the stool upside down and make a miniature bed of it, but it wasn't easy to make the cat lie still while she covered it up with her cardigan. Mostly though she'd just sit, poker in hand, shifting the white ash accumulating between the bars of the old-fashioned kitchen grate, revealing the glowing cinders like magic golden caves, caves with shadows moving in them like tormented bodies writhing in Hell. She could hear her father playing the piano in the upstairs sitting-room, 'Finlandia', 'Ave Maria', bits of Chopin and worst of all, 'Barcarolle'; that destroyed her completely. The sound coming from the damp, tiny, un-tuned piano that her father played so lovingly and so well (considering the difficulties) filled her with dread and fear: fear of the future, fear of the unknown, the supernatural, thunder and lightning, and of being grown up – what if she didn't get a husband – or worse still, got one, and had a barren womb like the woman in the Bible, or an illegitimate

* This true story was told to me by a Lewis maid we had from Bru Barvas (the West Side of the island).

167

baby, like Katie Ann in the village who hid it in the barn amongst the hay until it died . . . God forbid!

She looked quickly, guiltily towards Seònag Mairi Jean, afraid she might have read her thoughts. But no, Seònag Mairi Jean had thoughts of her own, sitting in the high-backed rocking-chair, rocking and knitting and letting great tears roll down her freckled apple cheeks. 'What's the matter, Seònag?' (She was aye greeting.)

'Nothing,' she sniffed, and brushed her cheek with the back of her hand.

'Tell me.'

'Och, I'm homesick.'

'You can't be, you've been here a month now. Are you sure it isn't the Barcarolle that's doing it to you? It does it to me.'

'What's that?'

'The thing my father's playing.'

'Ach no, I never noticed it, it's only the bagpipes that moves me.'

'What then? My mother's good to you isn't she? And you do like us, you've said so many times. It's not as though you've never been in service before. You went to England once, didn't you?'

'Dhia beannaich mi,* never again! I arrived with my tin trunk at the railway station, and there was not a soul meeting me; and worse still, when I found my way to the house there was no one in it, and me after travelling six hundred miles of boat and train from the back of Harris.'

'What did you do?'

* Dhia beannaich mi – God bless me

'Well, what could I do? It was a warm day, so I took off my hat, and my shoes and stockings, and sat on my trunk in the bit of a garden in front of the house, and started combing out my hair. After a while I felt the eyes of someone peering at me from an upstairs window of the next house. But when I looked up she dropped the screens, and I went on combing my hair, I combed it over my face making a wee slot that I could see through. She was still there all right. After a while I got fed up and parted my hair in the middle and pulled faces at her like this' (putting her thumbs to her nose and pulling down the corners of her eyes, she thrust out her tongue and went skelly. It was magnificent, like *The Hunchback of Notre Dame*).

'What did the woman do then?'

'Well, she screamed. You could hear her a mile away. Then she ran out of the house and fetched a policeman.'

'Gosh.'

'Yes, he came with his wee notebook and accused me of "loitering and obscene behaviour in public".

"What's your name?" he said.

"Seònag Mairi Jean."

"Sounds Greek to me. And address?"

"Bru Barvas, the Machair, Harris."

"There's no such place," he said. "You're nuts, and my name's not 'Arris." I was always scared of policemen anyway, since my brother got caught breaking the cups on the telegraph poles at home. They were just about to take me away to the clink, when my new mistress turned up. She'd got the dates mixed up, she said. She was a trash of a woman anyway, and I left there as soon as I'd saved enough money to get my fare home.'

'What's so special about home, anyway, Seònag, that you're always greeting to get back there?'

'Well, it's the time of year as much as anything, the spring, and the lambing.'

'The rain and the storms you mean,' said Sheena, glancing up at the window.

'Ach well, it's early yet. It's thundery, right enough, though.'

'I'm frightened of thunder and lightning. Are you?'

'And so well you might be, it's the wrath of God.'

'The wr*au*th of God.'

'The wrath of God – you and your English – I know what I'm talking about. There were two neighbours of ours living up in Barvas, bachelors they were, no woman would have them, you see. Amadans that's what they were and that foolish with the drink, putting the fear of death in everyone with their fighting and poaching and working on women. Holy terrors, both of them. They lived alone and did for themselves, if you could call it that, with the hens caching all over the place. Well, one stormy night, much the same as this with the rain pouring down and a storm brewing, they were sitting one on either side of the fire, like ourselves. The big one,* Seòras Mór, he was sitting with his feet up on the mantelpiece (he was a very tall man) and the wee one, Seòras Beag, he was leaning forward with his head in his hands (he had a wee spìdeag on him, if you know what I mean, what your father would call a hangover). There they were then, and the thunder had started, and the lightning was flashing, lighting the whole place up better than the Tilley lamp†.

* big one – older of the two
† Tilley lamp – pressurised metal lamp with mantle

When suddenly there was a crash like the heavens falling in, and a streak of lightning came skirling down the chimney between the two men. It took the boots off the one, Seòras Mór, and the scalp off the other, Seòras Beag, and neither one of them was killed. But from that day on you couldn't find a holier pair of men! They signed the pledge, and never touched another drop. Seòras Mór precents in the church and Seòras Beag takes round the plate. So you see, the Lord works in a mysterious way.'

Sheena moved her stool away from the fire and held the kitten close. 'Tell me more about Bru Barvas, Seònag,' she said, 'What do you do in summer?'

'Well, summer in our place it's the shieling, of course. If your mother will let me, I'll maybe take you with me sometime. Would you like that?'

'Oh yes, please do Seònag.'

'Maybe you'd be scared. There's lots of people get scared up there. It's very lonely and isolated, and it's not only the men they're scared of, though they're bad enough, God knows.'

'What then?'

'The unknown, apparitions and the like, spooky as Hell sometimes. I wouldn't like to be left alone like the poor woman that lost her man, after the others had all gone home.'

'Who? What? Tell me!'

'Well, it was this poor creature that had just recently got married and had built a good strong hut up at the shieling, intending to stay up there for a long spell with his new bride. It was more to get away from his mother-in-law than anything else, he couldn't abide her, we all knew that. However, after the grazing time was over, and the sheep all scattered, and the folk from the village all gone home, Tormod and his bride Raonaid remained on (for reasons best known to themselves, they were very much in love, you see). Well, as I was saying, one day while Tormod was mending the fencing round the hut, didn't he go and get a big rusty nail into his hand, between the thumb and his index finger. Raonaid bathed it, and they thought no more about it for a while, but towards nightfall, didn't his whole arm become discoloured and inflamed. Even then they didn't realise the seriousness of it, they were both so young and foolish, you see. By the time the fever got a hold of him it was too late to do anything. He clung to Raonaid while she struggled to bathe the sweat off him. What else could she do, poor creature? How could she leave him on the top of the mountains in the pitch blackness of the night? How could she even find her way back? She had no sense of direction and there was no doctor in the village, even if she got there. All she could do was hold him close when he shivered and swab his burning brow, and pray that God would show them a miracle. Now here's a strange thing: He did, though not in the way you think. The young man died, right enough, and Raonaid was as good as dead. What could she do with a corpse? After all, she was only nineteen and she had never even seen one, let alone – dress it, she had no linen, nothing, and a good two days' climbing between her and any kind of help. She collapsed in a heap in front of the hut and tore her fingernails into the earth. Goodness knows how long she lay there; then just when she began to feel her own spirit going, wafting away from her, she thought she felt a tap on her shoulder, soft as dust, and a tall man was standing beside her.

172

He was a complete stranger, she had never set eyes on him in her life before, and he didn't look like any other man; his clothes were much the same but himself was somehow different.

'"You must help me," he said. "Go, fetch water and follow me to the hut!" She did as he bid her without question. When she got inside, Tormod was laid out on the trust with his arms crossed on his breast, and he looked more beautiful than she had ever known him . . . She gazed, spellbound, till the man's voice said, "Fetch peat and build a fire, to last well on." Again she obeyed his command, and when she returned with a big load of peat she saw that her Tormod was swathed in white linen from head to toe. Well, where had he got it from? She had no linen.

'After what seemed like a long time, standing beside herself like floating under a calm sea, she felt the stranger's hands on her shoulders again. He was placing her cape round her. "We must go now," he said "I'll show you a path down the mountain."

'Now the funny thing was, he didn't seem to open his mouth when he spoke, his words seemed to come into her mind, unspoken. She knew, though, that she must do his bidding.

'After walking rough for some considerable time in the half darkness of the summer night, not feeling anything, just trusting her guide, the dawn began to break and she could see a path she never knew existed. She made towards it hurriedly, half running, or, as it seemed to her, sailing along. It seemed as though she were being pushed, her feet not touching the ground; then she came to a sudden halt and looked around for her companion. He'd gone, disappeared into space. She peered into the misty morning but couldn't see a sign of him. She sat waiting till it was full mid-morning sun. Then suddenly she could feel again and the fullness of her anguish came back on her; slowly she picked herself up and made along the path. Soon, sooner than she had thought possible, she saw the first of the cottages in the village and heard the rhythm of the looms, like the beat of her heart, clack-clack-clack . . . clack clack.

'She was half dead when she fell at her mother's feet; they could make no sense of what she tried to tell them. So the men went to see for themselves.'

'And did they find out who the stranger was?'

'No, never,' said Seònag, choking again with her tears, 'but in Bru Barvas, fine we know that he came from beyond the grave. Dhia beannaich sinn.'*

* Dhia beannaich sinn – God bless us

Communications

Walking along the Com A Tea Road (the Committee Road) and then up the Entry Mór (Big Entry) I stopped short when I came to the old well, its rusty bit of iron piping still directing the peat-brown water. And I looked up over the dyke to find Anna Cameron's house, but there was no sign of it, just a field of yellow buttercups, some dockens and a few stones still outlining the shape of what was once a charming thatched cottage with an overgrown path . . . and then I started to laugh. Laugh now as I did then at the sound of her raucous voice in my ears – of course she wasn't there – I only imagined I could hear her belching loud and clear at her cottage door, or halfway up the Entry on her way to the post office. Wherever she went you could never fail to hear her bellowing aloud in the Gaelic, 'O mar a tha mi leis a'ghaoith!' (Oh, how that I am with the wind) . . . and a tearing, earsplitting belch would follow as sure as night the day.

Anna was a spinster and she and her brother lived alone in the cottage. He had made all the furniture himself; the old pine beds with straw mattresses smelling of clover, the stools and chairs scarred and shiny with Donald's constant cutting and rolling of oily black twist tobacco on them, the leather canopy round the chimney (with sometimes the half of a sheep's carcass hanging on a great iron hook to cure in the smoke). The peat and wood fire was set in the mud floor – I would grope my way in there as a small child – making towards the light of the fire, its smoke wafting as much through the door as up the chimney.

'What's wrong with your chimney?' I'd ask.

'Ach, it's those scholars throwing cabbages down it on their way home from the school,' grumbled Donald.

Once when I went, the old man told me that Anna was ill; he had got the doctor to her. 'What did he recommend?' I asked.

'Ach, he told me to put a poultice on her chest, and then when he came again he looked for the poultice in her blouse. "It's not there," I said, "it's where you told me to put it – on her chest – over there, man, on the chest of drawers." He is a fool of a man anyway,' continued Donald. 'Didn't he want me to get her some cocoa. Well, I bought her a tin of the stuff at the post office, but they didn't tell me how to make it.'

'Put it in a bowl, the same way as you make the brose,' bellowed Anna between bouts of wind, 'pour some boiling water on it and cover it with a saucer, then leave it to stand.' How she ever ate it God only knows!

Now, Anna had another brother away in the army, and she used to struggle up the hill to the P.O. with parcels for him. But as she got older the parcels seemed to get heavier and her mind and her body got weaker, so she asked Donald, 'What about sending them by telegraph, the poles are far handier than the post office?' So the next day she hung a box of eggs on the nearest telegraph pole, and the next time she passed it had gone, and she felt very pleased with herself. So she hung a pair of new boots up and the following morning there was an old pair in place of them! 'It was a fine way of communication,' thought Anna.

Then one day the doctor told her that most of the lads from the village were reported missing, including her younger brother. 'How could that be?' she said. 'It's not true; I know well enough, because he is still getting the parcels from me!'

'How do you know that?' asked the doctor kindly.

'Well, he sent his old boots back to be repaired, they were hanging on the telegraph pole covered in mud. It must be an awful mucky place this Flanders.'

'And there must a very lucky tinker going around somewhere,' thought the doctor . . .

It was hard indeed to drag myself away from this yellow field where I could laugh or belch out loud if I wanted to.

Gaynor my Guide Dog

The old woman walks every day now along the white path. She loves that white path, she feels so secure. She won't get run over by any traffic because no traffic can go along it. It's very narrow and it's very white, consisting of marble chippings from the nearby marble quarry at Elgol. This path was recently made, and it runs right round the Broadford Bay till it reaches the old pier. The old pier where the steamers used to come in once upon a time followed by dolphins, and one could see the odd whale tossing and spurting in the bay. But all these large fish seem to have been frightened away, particularly since the new bridge has been built linking the Isle of Skye with the mainland. This has brought so much more traffic to the island, and the place is no longer a peaceful paradise, or so thinks the old lady.

She's beginning to get out of breath, and walking without being able to see is not easy, everything is in shadow. Tall wild flowers can sometimes look like human beings and give one quite a fright. She's not alone, of course, because she is the proud possessor of a wonderful guide dog, a great big black dog – fully trained, a delightful creature, a half-breed – half collie and half retriever. The old lady's thinking about the days she's spent in this same bay when she was young, how she used to go swimming every morning with her father; and thinking how much she loves it here, and doesn't now want to go anywhere else. She is fully content, but, oh dear me, so out of breath and so tired!

But soon she will reach a huge granite rock, and there she can go and sit and rest herself. Her feet in springtime down amongst the golden buttercups. Not that she can see the golden buttercups but she knows they're there. She has all seasons in her memory, the early spring, the summer and the winter. And now she's remembering how a good many years ago in the middle of winter, rather, in January, when there was the most fantastic frost and snowstorms and it was almost impossible to get out of the house. But she'd decided rather late in the day, round about four o'clock, to take her guide dog, or rather for her guide dog to take her for a walk. There was no white path in those days.

So she went up to the high road that led past Corry Lodge and all the way to the Irishman's Point, an outcrop of rocks some three miles away or more. It was very difficult to walk because there was an awful lot of ice about, everything was frozen stiff. But with Gaynor, that was the name of her guide dog, she could hold on to the harness and feel fairly safe . . . (Now I had better come clean and tell you, this is really a true story, about my own experience, for the old woman is what I call myself and Gaynor is my own guide dog.) So I progressed for some three and a half miles this late winter's day towards the said Irishman's Point, when suddenly and un-expectedly I slid and fell, and the pain was exquisite. I had fallen onto a rock that was protruding out of the ice on the rugged path. I had given Gaynor a free run; she had gone galloping down to the seashore in pursuit of a rubber ball which she liked to flick with her nose into the edge of the sea and then retrieve it. Gaynor was very remarkably good at this and was having huge fun. But quite uncannily, she sensed that there was something wrong with the old lady. And she left her ball on the shore and raced up to the old girl who was lying semi-conscious on the ice. So she turned her backside towards the lady's head and waved her tail over the old girl's face backwards and forwards, backwards and forwards. And every now and then the old girl would regain consciousness and realise that she had a whistle round her neck. The whistle was meant for retrieving the dog. So she blew . . . whistling and shouting was to no avail . . .

The sound of the sea which was fast coming in was drowning my voice and drowning the sound of the whistle (though long afterwards I learned that a whistle had been heard, but the people in the nearest house had thought that it was Nigel the shepherd who was rounding up his sheep). In my semi-conscious state I was hearing music, lovely music like that of Mendelssohn. And then there would be a kind of thud, and I realised or thought I'd realised that I was floating on a wave and being bashed against a rock, and it was agony. And then the waves would start to recede and I would be back again on the water floating along like a seagull on the surface. And so it went on. All the time I was managing to have a miraculous grip on Gaynor's long hair that grew all over her backside in profusion, thank God. And she diligently dragged me on the thick ice along the path, till eventually she dragged me up onto the high road the way we had come.

And it so happened that the Broadford Hospital was built on the side of the high road. Well, I don't know how the dog knew that it was a hospital. How could she know that it was a hospital? Perhaps she realised or could smell all the medicaments and anaesthetics and things, and it reminded her of the vets that had previously attended to her as a puppy and throughout her life. At any rate she halted at the Broadford Hospital gate, and I regained consciousness enough to yell once more. And she proceeded to bark; eventually someone arrived and got me into the hospital, and they operated on a dislocated shoulder that same night.

It had taken three long hours to be pulled by Gaynor, who never left me for one instant. It was an absolute miracle. In the morning they discovered that I had also broken my leg. Gaynor had never left the front of the hospital gates all night. And in the morning the nurses or the matron or someone got in touch with my next of kin, who happened to be a cousin, and she came and collected Gaynor and took her home with her. And she would be very very good to her. I was placed in an ambulance and motored that long long distance from Skye to Inverness to Raigmore Hospital. There I was put in intensive care and my leg was operated on, and I still have the tin plate and the screws which they put it together with.

When I was well enough they put me into a proper ward with six other beds, or five other beds, and somebody had discovered, mainly through cards I'd received from Skye and from various friends, that it was my birthday, my eightieth birthday. And believe it or not the hospital made me a cake and sent it up to our ward, a huge big cake! And I happened to be wearing a sort of square box for monitoring my heart affixed round my waist. So I decided that it would be great fun to have a party, and I got another cousin to go to Marks and Spencer and buy a case of wine.

So we had a great party in the ward and I was feeling rather happy and in much less pain, so I pretended to be a bus conductress, and I tore up all my cards into little oblong pieces, and clicked them on my heart monitoring machine, and handed them to each of the patients before they would be given a hunk of cake and a glass of wine. But I can tell you, even though everyone was extremely good to me, I was indeed glad to get home to Skye and to be once more greeted by my faithful, wonderful dog. Gaynor is the best, the very best, and I thought you should know about it.

Editor's Note

The vernacular Island English, overlaid with vibrant colloquial Gaelic, strong Scots and witty slang is a rich vein of expression for story. The Gaelic shown in the text of *Consider an Island* is not modern, but rather the language as it is pronounced in South Skye. For the benefit of interested non-Gaelic readers, a very basic Guide to Pronunciation has been provided. Phrases in Gaelic are translated in the text, exactly as Rhona wrote and read them in her broadcasts. The odd words that are not defined in the stories have been placed in a Glossary. Some folklore has been added to the stories as footnotes where relevant. One narrative, 'Skye's the Limit', has been altered from the original BBC transcription, replacing the final commentary on Skye's popular culture with the novelty of Grandmother Mackinnon.

Dr John MacInnes, Scotland's eminent Gaelic scholar has acclaimed the narrative:

> Mrs Rauszer's writing is absolutely charming. She has a light touch and her very attractive brand of humour pervades her work. Her style is never dull, never ponderous. Most if not all of the stories were broadcast and are patently designed for reading aloud . . . One is conscious throughout of the tones and of the living voice. This cannot ever fail to give a buoyancy to the writer's style.

Fifteen stories in this collection, *Consider an Island*, were previously recorded for BBC Scottish Home Service transmission. They are (in order of occurrence):

'To School in Skye', BBC recording no. TGW 61364, transmitted on *Listen Awhile* 2/1964
'Father on the Island', tape no. 1/GW/59566; *Listen Awhile* 10/1963
'Septimus', BBC Aberdeen *Town and Country* 4/1967 and BBC Glasgow 7/1967, prod. A P Lee
'Chains', BBC Aberdeen *Town and Country* 5/1968, prod. A Rogers
'Mare's Tail', BBC Aberdeen *Town and Country* 4/1967 and *A Few Stories and Songs from the Highlands and Islands* 6&9/1967
'Helik Stag', BBC Aberdeen *Town and Country* 9/1965 and BBC London 7/1966
'Flight of Fancy' BBC *Town and Country Magazine* 2/1967; BBC London and Glasgow 7/1967, prod. A P Lee
'Windfall', BBC Aberdeen 7/1967 (?)
'The Pied Piper', BBC London 9/1966 and Aberdeen, *A Few Stories and Songs from the Scottish Highlands and Islands* 6&9/1967
'The Ring on the Tree', BBC London 7/1966; BBC Aberdeen, *Home this Afternoon* 4/1967 and *Town and Country* 6/1967
'The Magic Willow', BBC Aberdeen *Town and Country* 9/1965 and BBC London 7/1966
'The Kittens', BBC Aberdeen *Town and Country* 9/1965 and BBC London 7/1966
'The Corn Cailleach', BBC Aberdeen *Town and Country* 9/1965 and BBC London 7/1966

'Skye's the Limit' rec. no. TGW 66392, BBC Glasgow *Listen Awhile* 12/1964
'Silver Strands', BBC Glasgow 10/1981 (?)

The balance of the present collection is to our knowledge unpublished.

Guide to Pronunciation

Vowels	*English sound equivalent*	*Gaelic examples*
a	short like *a* in *cat*	stad, cramachan
à	long like *a* in *far*	bàn, slàinte
e	short like *e* in *get*	e, le, Fergus
é	long like *a* in *fame*	dé, té
i	short like *i* in *king*, or *e* in *me*;	sin; bi, mi tigh
	short like *i* in *tight* (one word only)	tigh
ì	long like *e* in *feet*	spìdeag
o	short like *o* in *modest*	mo, bochans
ò	long like *a* in *awe*	Òrdag
ó	long like *o* in *bold*	mór
u	long like *oo* in *poor*	pushag, currac

Consonants

b	at beginning of word like *b* in *boat*; elsewhere like *p* in *captive*	Bru Barvas, bodach; sgriob
bh	at beginning and end like *v*; in middle of word often silent	Bhic, obh; Liubhrais
c	at beginning like *c* in *can*; in middle or end like *chk*	cladach; plucean, mic
ch	as *ch* in *loch* (never *ch* in cheer)	cha, cailleach, Sligachan
chd	like *ch* with *k* added	buidseachd
d	at beginning like *d* in *drew*; elsewhere like *t* in *cattle*; before *e* or *i* like *j* in *jet*	Domhnall, Dunan; Òrdag, Sad; dé, dearbh, Dia
dh	gutteral like *ch* but less explosive before or after *a*, *o*; before or after *e*, *i* like *y* in *yield*; at end of word silent	dhan; Dhia; tapadh, ceilidh, Seonaidh

f	as in English	Fearchar, falbh
fh	at beginning of word silent	Fhearchar
g	at beginning or before *a, o, u* like *g* in *go*; elsewhere like *ck* in *neck*	gu, agad; stapag Neilag
gh	before or after *i, e* like *y* in *yield*; in middle and at end of words silent as in *night*	a' ghealach, gheallaidh; nighean, briagh
l	similar to *l* in *lure*; darker next to *a, o, u*	leisgeadair, mil'; slàinte, mol, Giorsal
ll	flanked by *i* and *e* like *ll* in *million*; otherwise like *ll* in *pull*	cailleach; Caillich, Cuillins
m	like *m* in English	machair, Tormod
mh	at beginning and end like *v* in English; in middle generally silent	mhic; sàmhach
n	similar to English; before *e, i* like *n* in *not*; after *c, g, m, t* usually like *r*	an, na; nighean; cnoc
nn	flanked by *a, o, u* like *ion* in *onion*	beannaich
p	like *p* in English	pushag
r	like English, with more of a roll	sgriob, mór
rt	as *rst* or *rsht*	ort
s	before or after *a, o, u* like English *ss*; before or after *e, i* like *sh*	sagart, às; sin, seabhas, uist, Breacais
sh	at beginning of word is like *h*	shin, shis
t	before or after *a, o, u* like *t* in *tone*; before or after *e, i* like *ch* in *chin*	Tormod, crotal; té, fàilte, slàinte
th	at beginning often like *h* in *hat*, but can be silent; in middle silent *Combinations* of *lb, lch, lm, lp* interpolate a drawl vowel between them	tha, Thighearna; thu, thusa, latha falbh, Balbhan, Scalpay

Diphthongs

ai	short like *i* in *thin*, or *e* in *red*, the *i* silent;	air, ainm, cailleach
	at end of word before *dh* like *i* in *thin*;	achaidh, gheallaidh, slabhraidh
	at end of word before *d*, like *itch*	Raonaid, Ealasaid

ài	long like *a* in *father*, the *i* silent	slàinte, fàilte, Màiri
ao	between English *oo* and *ee*	naoimh, ghaoil, glaoich
ea	like *e* in *red*, sometimes *ya* in *yacht*	beag, Earreigh; bealach, each, Ealasaid, Beathag
éi	like *a* in *fate*;	céilidh, éirich;
ei	like *i* in *thin*;	Blàbheinn, leibh eilean
eo	*e* slightly sounded and *o* as in *modest*	Eoghann, Seonaid, Seòras, Macleod
ia, io	*ee-a* as in *me-and*-you	Dia, cioch, Giorsal
iu	*i* very short, *u* as in *poor*	Liubhrais
oi	as *a* in *awe*	a' Choire
ua	short *u* like in *fully*, *a* obscure	ruadh
ui	*u* long like *oo* in *poor*, *i* silent	buidseachd, Cuillins, cuidich

Glossary

Gaelic words, 'G'; Scots words, 'Sc'; Slang, 'Sl'; from, 'f';
compare, 'cf'

ag	– feminine diminutive termination (G)
Aiseag	– ferry (G)
almightiness, the	– gift from God, second sight
amadan	– fool, rascal (G)
amn't	– am not (Sc)
an	– the (G)
aye	– always (Sc)
Balbhan, the	– dumb person (G)
banshee	– f ban-sìthe (G), disaster fairy
besom	– broom; contemptuous woman (Sc)
b(h)eag	– little; younger (G)
bealach	– pass of a mountain, glen; gateway (G)
biscuit, ship's	– thick, hard, caraway cake from abroad
Blàbheinn	– highest mountain of the Strathaird peninsula, South Skye (G)
bleezag	– small bonfire, f bleeze (Sc)
bochans	– booths, huts, where men gathered and slept (G)
bobby dazzler	– brilliant eye-catcher (Sl)
brose	– dish of meal mixed with boiling water or milk (Sc)
buidseachd	– a spell; cf buitseachas (G), witchcraft
bumailear	– bungler (G)
caching	– dropping (their) turds (Sc)
cailleach	– old woman (G)
Cairistiona	– Christina (G)
Cartogena	– name of Spanish city brought back by Highland soldiers from Peninsular War, 1809; name of the cailleach

céilidh	– visit for news, story, song (G)
cioch	– woman's breast, pap (G)
cladach	– shore, beach (G)
click	– suitor, boyfriend (Sl)
cohannia	– Polish form of general endearment
Coruisk	– Loch Coruisk in the Cuillin Hills; cauldron of water (G)
cramachan	– butter churn (G)
creel	– a deep basket for carrying peats, fish, etc on the back
crotal	– orangey-brown; dark red dye made from boiling moss off the rocks (G)
Cuillins	– mountains of Minginish, South Skye (G)
currac	– woman's cap, mutch (G)
Curstag	– Kirsty (G)
Dhia, dia	– God (G)
doh-re-mi . . .	– tonic sol-fa scale
Dougie	– f Dougal (G), dark stranger
dram	– a measure of whisky (Sc)
drink, the	– the sea (Sl)
Eachann	– Hector (G)
Ealasaid	– Elizabeth (G)
Earreigh, an	– Earrach (G), Spring (season)
éirich	– rise! (G)
Eoghan	– Ewen (G)
fàilte	– welcome (G)
fank	– f fang (G), sheep pen
fey	– other-worldly, fatal (Sc)
gemmer	– familiar name for a gamekeeper (Sc); cf geamair (G)
Gift (the)	– second sight (God-given)
gheallaidh	– f gealach (G), moon; party
glaoich	– idiot (G)
glengarries	– flat-sided caps or bonnets (Sc)
greeting	– weeping (Sc)
gruel	– porridge, food made of oatmeal (Sc)
haywire (went)	– crazy
helik	– cf halloch (Sc), uncouth
humdinger	– anything superlatively good (Sl)
Iain	– John (G)
keek	– peep (Sc)
leisgeadair	– lazy one (G)

long johns	– men's long-legged underwear (Sl)
machair	– grasslands above shoreline (G)
Minch, the	– very unpredictable ocean passage between Skye and the Outer Hebrides
m(h)ór	– big; older (G)
namby-pambied	– f namby-pamby, weakly sentimental
Nellie, your	– life (Sl) (short for Nellie Duff)
obh obh	– och aye! alas (G)
pitterem-pattering	– learning pipe tunes with Gaelic vocables
plucean	– large clod of earth; pimple (G)
poit-mhùin	– chamber-pot (G)
pushag	– pussy, f puiseag (G)
Raonaid	– Rachel
rock salmon	– cured fish resembling salmon
ruadh	– reddish, red-haired (G)
Sad, a Mhic an	– Son of the Devil (G)
Sagart, an	– Priest (G)
Sassenach	– Englishman
scarletty-orange	– cf *scarlatto* (Italian), scarlet
seabhas	– wandering, labour (G)
Seadan	– the postman (G)
Seonaid	– Janet (G)
Seòras	– George (G)
seventeen-pointer	– big-headed stag
shaws	– stalks (Sc)
shenanigan	– cf seunaidhean (G), act of defending by charms or enchantment
shieling	– high remote summer pasture
shinty	– Highland game like field hockey (Sc)
shis	– cf shush
shoogled	– rocked (Sc)
shooshed	– f shoo
sick	– throw-up, vomit
skelly	– squint-eyed (Sc)
skirling	– crackling (Sc)
skyte	– slither, skid (Sc)
slabhraidh	– pot-hanger above the fire (G)
slàinte	– toast, health (G)
smalls	– underclothes (Sl)
smoorings	– smouldering embers (f smoor (Sc), to damp down a fire)
spate	– a flood (Sc)

spìdeag	– hangover (G)
splosher	– cf spailp (G), kiss
sporran	– f sporan (G), purse; leather money pouch worn in front of a man's kilt (Sc)
stapag	– mixure of meal and cream, milk or cold water (G)
stirks	– young cattle (Sc)
stoup	– wooden post (Sc)
stravaiging	– cf srabhaiche (G), like a straw, scattered; wandering about
stramash	– uproar (Sc)
swee	– moveable iron bar over a fire on which to hang pots and kettles (Sc)
Talisker	– famous Skye whisky
tawse	– five-fingered, leather punishment strap (Sc)
telling	– warning, admonition, lesson (Sc)
theirself	– themselves (Sc)
tishied	– stirred up, f *atisier* (Old French)
tourie	– rising to a point (Sc)
trust	– long wooden seat; f truis (G), gather, tuck up; cf trus-àite (G), blanket kist
twist	– thick cord of tobacco
Tormod	– Norman (G)
uist	– be quiet, hush! (G)
water kelpie	– demonic water horse (Sc)
weans	– small children, f wee anes (Sc)
weirdie	– odd, different (Sc)